EVERTON MILES IS STRANGER THAN ME

by

Philippa Dowding

DUNDURN
TORONTO

Editor: Allister Thompson
Design: Courtney Horner
Cover design: Courtney Horner
Cover image: background: Kathy Konkle/iStock, Shoes: Mikateke/iStock
Printer: Webcom

Library and Archives Canada Cataloguing in Publication

Dowding, Philippa, 1963-, author
    Everton Miles is stranger than me / Philippa Dowding.

(The night flyer's handbook)
Issued in print and electronic formats.
ISBN 978-1-4597-3527-9 (paperback).--ISBN 978-1-4597-3528-6 (pdf).--
ISBN 978-1-4597-3529-3 (epub)

    I. Title.

PS8607.O9874E94 2016   jC813'.6   C2016-901737-0
                                     C2016-901738-9

1 2 3 4 5   20   19 18 17 16

  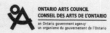

Conseil des Arts du Canada   Canada Council for the Arts   Canada   ONTARIO ARTS COUNCIL / CONSEIL DES ARTS DE L'ONTARIO / an Ontario government agency / un organisme du gouvernement de l'Ontario

We acknowledge the support of the **Canada Council for the Arts** and the **Ontario Arts Council** for our publishing program. We also acknowledge the financial support of the **Government of Canada** through the **Canada Book Fund** and **Livres Canada Books**, and the **Government of Ontario** through the **Ontario Book Publishing Tax Credit** and the **Ontario Media Development Corporation**.

Care has been taken to trace the ownership of copyright material used in this book. The author and the publisher welcome any information enabling them to rectify any references or credits in subsequent editions.

— *J. Kirk Howard, President*

The publisher is not responsible for websites or their content unless they are owned by the publisher.

Printed and bound in Canada.

VISIT US AT
Dundurn.com | @dundurnpress
Facebook.com/dundurnpress | Pinterest.com/dundurnpress

Dundurn
3 Church Street, Suite 500
Toronto, Ontario, Canada
M5E 1M2

EVERTON MILES IS STRANGER THAN ME

OTHER NIGHT FLYERS HANDBOOKS

The Strange Gift of Gwendolyn Golden

For Paul,
a Night Flyer from the start

Congratulations, your life as a Night Flyer starts today. We hope you find this copy of *Your First Flight: A Night Flyer's Handbook, The Complete & Unabridged Version (Newly Updated!)* a valuable reference for any questions you may have about Night Flying.

Do NOT lose it! This will be your only copy.

For quick and handy reference, here are Your Ten Most Pressing Questions Answered:

1. What is happening to me? You are, in all probability, a young teenager from a family of Night Flyers (except in very rare circumstances), and you have recently flown without mechanical assistance, which means that you have had your First Flight. You have therefore been identified by the local authorities (see Mentor and Watcher entries, below) as a Night Flyer. Rest assured that you are normal in every way, except now you have the added ability of unaided flight.

2. What is a Night Flyer? A Night Flyer is anyone (although most often a young teenager or adolescent entering puberty) who has taken his or her First Flight. The First Flight usually occurs in a safe and controlled manner with the young Night Flyer's parents, Watcher, and Mentor cheering him or her on. It is a time for celebration and joy.

3. Is Night Flying dangerous? Generally, no. Ask your Mentor for further instruction.

4. How do I control my flying? As noted in Question #2, Night Flying, or the ability to fly, usually begins during puberty, although sometimes much later, and except in a few very rare cases, almost never before. Since puberty is a time of great hormonal flux, you may find that you fly when you least want to, such as at times of stress, anger, sudden upset, or joy. Sometimes you may fly simply during a moment of boredom or carelessness. Young Night Flyers generally outgrow this troubling problem quickly. With practice, focus on breathing techniques, and the help of their Mentor, most Flyers gain control of their flight patterns within a few days or weeks after their First Flight.

5. How do I tell my friends? In most cases, the Night Flyer need not tell anyone except family members and other Flyers about his or her new ability. The decision to tell non-flying friends and community members must be made very carefully and often is not recommended. This is because in many, many unfortunate cases, non-flying prejudice has occurred. Extreme caution and restraint is advised, although there are no rules that forbid revealing the truth. Seek advice and wisdom from your Mentor.

6. What is a Watcher? One who watches, keeps watch, or is especially vigilant as a sentry or night guard. S/he is someone who is well-known to

the Flyer and who is constantly on the lookout for his or her First Flight and continued welfare. The Watcher is generally also a Flyer, but this is not essential. The Watcher and Mentor must work together well. The Watcher must take an oath to Watch faithfully.

7. What is a Mentor? A Mentor is steadfast, honourable, courageous. S/he is there to teach, guide, and help the young Night Flyer in every facet of his or her learning. The Mentor is not, in most cases, a family member, but is instead a member of the young Flyer's community. The Mentor/First Flyer relationship is usually one of great respect that often lasts into adulthood and beyond. The Mentor must take an oath to teach and guide faithfully. It is a sacred trust.

8. What ceremonies and parties do I attend? As a Night Flyer with full privileges, you may now attend the First Flight Ceremonies of any other Night Flyers in your community. You may also attend the annual Midsummer Party. Ask your Mentor for further information regarding the latter.

9. Can I lead a normal life? Generally, yes. Ask your Mentor for further instruction.

10. How many Night Flyers are there? The Night Flyer population rises and falls each day.

Five Full Privileges of a Night Flyer (Appendix D):

1. You may now fly unrestricted day* or night, at your discretion. (*Daytime flight is not generally recommended in populated areas.)
2. You have received your golden feather. You will receive only one. Keep it safe.
3. You now have a Watcher and a Mentor who have each taken an oath on your behalf.
4. You may attend all Night Flying ceremonies as a member with full privileges.
5. You must choose.

ONE

I'm flying.

It's 3:00 a.m.

I glide, effortless, over the rooftops and church spires of my little town. I float over the park that Jez and I meet at when we sneak out at night. The empty swings creak in the gentle last-night-of-summer breeze. I drift over the wooded lot next to the park then float slowly above empty streets. The back-yards, driveways, and rooftops pass below me like a miniature village, a child's play-world.

Past the library, I drift lazily over The Float Boat, the only candy store in town. Mrs. Forest, my Mentor, and her husband are tucked up inside, cozy against the night. My school, Bass Creek Senior Public School, drifts below me.

Correction. My OLD school. Tomorrow, I start high school at the big building further down the street.

No. I'm not flying over the high school tonight. Tomorrow will come soon enough.

So I pick up speed. I'm still not great at flying, to be honest, but I can finally go where I want, although I may never get the hang of landing. The fence tops and tree limbs float below me until I reach the last street in town. I hover and look out over the September cornfields toward the distant woods.

There's a solitary cabin at the edge of the forest. It belongs to Mr. McGillies, a local hermit, the old bottle collector who has sworn an oath to be my Watcher when I'm out flying. The truth is he saved my life recently, and I don't know how to thank him. I've been drawn to this spot all summer, watching the shape of his dark cabin against the forest as I bob above the corn like a weather balloon.

Tonight though, something is different.

I gaze past his cabin, past the trees, out toward the glow of faraway city lights. Somewhere out there the oldest trees stand. Somewhere out there the Spirit Flyers wait, starshot immortals, guardians of light and air.

Then something flashes in the muddy laneway below me.

A small lost thing lies face-up in the mud. I drop and hover above the road to investigate. It's a tiny figure, a doll made of cornstalks. It stares up at me with bright glass beads for eyes.

This is odd. Who would put a doll in the laneway like this? What child would have visited Mr. McGillies and lost it? None, since he never has visitors as far as I know. With one hand I clasp my father's golden feather on my mother's chain around my neck.

With the other I reach down to touch the doll, but then I swear the corn rustles next to me and a voice whispers: *Gwendolyn.*

I zoom up above the corn.

Gwendolyn.

The corn has never whispered to me before. Then a lone figure steps out of the field onto the muddy lane. It hesitates then takes a step toward me. A dark figure with glowing golden eyes.

And wings.

Gwendolyn.

I streak home and dive into my bed.

I don't know what I just saw, but I do know this: from somewhere out there, a darkness is coming.

And it's calling my name.

TWO

Jeffrey Parks begins to cry.

We all immediately look away, humiliated for him.

We're sitting in the first few minutes of the very first day of grade nine. We'll be playing this scenario out for the rest of the year, the rest of high school, the rest of our lives. From now on whenever we think of grade nine, this will be our first thought: Jeffrey Parks cried on the first day.

Mortification fills my every pore.

Our homeroom teacher, Mrs. Mayhew, is loud. She's a slammer and a pointer. She already slammed the door and made the windows rattle, then loudly demanded that Jeffrey Parks tell everyone what he did all summer. I think she's just trying to get us to introduce ourselves, but she's so loud that we've all gone to ground like frightened birds.

I glance at Jez next to me. This would never have been allowed in Bass Creek Senior Public School, us sitting together, since we talk too much. I have to tell her about the whispers in the corn, the dark, winged figure in the laneway last night, but I'm too scared of Mrs. Mayhew to try. I haven't told her yet, since I'm the only teenager in the world without a phone, and anyone can listen in on our home phone.

We all stare at the back of Jeffrey Parks's exposed neck because unlike all sensible people, he's sitting at the front of the class. We simply can't look away. Even the huge boys who grew gigantic over the summer, with legs that stick out like a grasshopper's beneath their desks. Even the girls from nearby small towns, girls I don't know, which is most of them.

We all just stare.

Mrs. Mayhew stands over Jeffrey Parks. He looks like he's stopped crying, but I can't be sure. At least, I don't see his shoulders shake like they did a minute ago. His knuckles are white where he grips the desk.

"Well? What *did* you do this summer?" Mrs. Mayhew looks at her clipboard. "Jeffrey Parks," she adds for emphasis.

Come on, Jeffrey! I think. *Give her an answer! I'm sorry for booting you and making you cry in grade five, but it should have made you tougher. If you go down now, we're all lost.* But Jeffrey just folds like there's no fight in him. His head goes down on his desk. Mrs. Mayhew looks puzzled, then almost kind, like she wants to help but doesn't know how.

"Okay, Mr. Parks, never mind," she says and then goes on to call out the rest of our names. When the bell rings, we all file out to start the first full day of grade nine, and Jeffrey never does lift his head off the desk. I watch the pulse in the back of his exposed neck as I hurry past. I wish I could say I stopped to say a comforting word, but I'd be lying. I file by like everyone else, trying not to let his tears rub off on me.

All I can think as I pass by is: *Someone has to fall on the first day, Gwendolyn. Just be thankful it's not you.*

THREE

I navigate to my locker, something I've never had before.

There's no way to do this locker thing with dignity. I pin books under my chin and get the combination wrong. Again. Jez breezes up beside me and opens her locker one-handed, like she's been doing it her whole life. Jez is going to be good at high school. She was born to be a cheerleader, to wear the right clothes, to be at ease with everyone. Jez will never struggle at her locker.

"Jeffrey Parks's parents got divorced this summer," she says with a little whiff of superiority. "That's why he was crying." She slips her books onto the locker shelf.

"Oh," I say. Poor Jeffrey. My locker door suddenly escapes and swings wide. The boy on the other side of me jumps. The kid stares at me. Even his braces look scared.

"Sorry," I mumble. I don't know him but maybe he's already heard about me. I slam my locker shut. I do have a reputation for having a bad temper. Then there's this whole vicious rumour thing, too. The town was convinced I was a drug addict. Long story.

But I'm not, believe me. I hate drugs.

The kid bolts, and for a second Jez and I are alone. I should tell my best friend that someone … something … is at the edge of town calling my name. But I don't. Everyone is between classes and the halls are packed. It's too noisy to talk. Besides, what am I going to say that doesn't sound like I made it up? And what did I see anyway? Probably nothing.

But this is the very first time I've kept a secret from Jez. She knows absolutely everything there is to know about me. She was the first person to find out I'm a Night Flyer, for instance (followed by Mr. McGillies, Mrs. Forest, then my mother).

We push our way through the halls like salmon swimming upstream to gym class. We find the girl's locker room, then we mill around with the other grade nine girls.

I scan the gym, which is easy since I'm one of the tallest, but there's no one else I know.

Until *she* appears. Shelley Norman.

My bully.

Shelley Norman strides into gym with the other grade ten girls. I grab Jez.

"What's SHE doing here?" I hiss. How can this be happening? I put up with Shelley Norman in gym classes in middle school. But now?

"Not enough girls in grade ten take gym. Jeesh, Gwen."

Shelley Norman has tree trunks for legs, and she's grown about six inches since I saw her last spring. She's a giant. She marches into the gym, and it really doesn't matter who else is in the room. I'm the only person she sees. Our eyes lock.

There's a sloppiness to Shelley. She needs a good scrub or something. Her shorts have a smear of ketchup and what might be egg on them, and it's just the first day. I think of my mother carefully teaching me how to do the laundry a few years ago, and I wonder who let Shelley have such filthy shorts.

I gulp. I slowly feel my stupid mouth curl up at the edges in terror, but from Shelley's point of view it must look like a weird grin. I will my lips to do a downturn, but it's too late. Shelley laughs. She turns to her friends and whispers, and they all turn and laugh at me.

I look away. Just standing in gym is now an ordeal. All I really want to do is bolt.

Or fly away.

Our teacher, Miss Moreau, walks in and I spend the rest of the class trying to keep clear of Shelley's dodgeball. But it's no use. She hits me every time. I'm already black and blue, and it's only the first day.

There's a grade nine assembly at the end of the day. It's dull, but there's one hilarity in the form of Mr. Skinty, our principal. He's the skinniest man I've ever seen. He's Mr. Skinny. Or worse, Mr. Stinky (although I'm too far away to detect any odours). I'm desperately trying not to giggle, when suddenly a face pops out of the crowd a few rows down.

I've been dreading this moment.

It's Martin Evells. He raises his hand in a weak hello. I've been trying not to see Martin all day, trying to forget that he goes to this school, or that he exists at all.

I don't wave back. Instead I stare straight ahead at skeletal, stinky Mr. Skinty.

Martin was my best friend when I was six.

He's the boy whose mother phoned the police on me, whose mother started the vicious "drug addict" rumour about me. And he's also the boy who gave me the Worst Kiss Ever last spring.

Martin and I will have to talk sometime, I can see that.

Honestly, I'd rather die.

FOUR

Jez and I walk home. Older kids jostle past us on the sidewalk. Now is the perfect time to tell her about the winged creature calling my name last night.

But for some strange, sneaky reason, I don't. It's too weird. And what was it, anyway?

Instead, we talk about day one in high school. About Shelley Norman and terrible cafeteria food and poor Jeffrey Parks. Then Jez walks off down her street and I wander on alone. This is the one day all year I don't have to pick up my little twin brother and sister, Christine and Christopher (the Chrissies if I'm mad at them, C2 if I'm not), after school. Mom always picks them up on the first day, but from now on it'll be my job. There's no one else to share the parenting, just me and Mom.

Now you're wondering why. Don't. Dad vanished, disappeared, died, whatever you want to call it, in a terrible storm a few weeks before the twins were born. He was a Night Flyer too (but Mom's not), and for some stupid reason he was checking on a neighbour.

I was six.

Now you know.

When I open my front door, noise hits me like a wall. The twins roar around the living room shrieking into each other's faces.

Christine shouts, "Mrs. Norton is so smelly, I can't even get close to her. She's RE-PELL-ANT!"

Christopher shouts back, "Just hold your nose!" They're in grade two and this year their principal, Mrs. Abernathy, got the bright idea that they should be in separate classes. "For their development as individuals," she said to my mother on the phone a few weeks before school started.

My mother worried about this. The twins are spectacularly twinned. They think together, they finish each other's sentences, and sometimes I swear they brain-talk to each other. They have the same name, also a bad idea, but no one listened to me when they were born. Jez thinks they're weird, and sometimes I have to agree.

I really can't say what will happen to them if they're separated all day. The first inkling, this screaming, is not good. They shriek and slam cupboards and bang dishes on the table. Mom hears me come in and calls hello from upstairs. Why isn't she calming them down?

"Mom! Why are C2 screaming?"

"Oh!" she calls back, like it's the first time she's noticed. "Could you feed them please, Gwen? I'm just finishing some work." My mom works for a law firm, and she just got a promotion. I sigh. My old dog, Cassie, is curled up on the couch, so I bury my

face in her smelly dog fur and she thumps her tail a
little. She doesn't even get up.

In the hall, I see a creamy yellow envelope on the
table. It has my name on it in elegant writing.

Gwendolyn Golden.

I frown and get a little knot in my stomach. I slip
the envelope into my back pocket then wade into
the kitchen. I order C2 to sit and *shhhh.* Bagels and
milk appear, which seems to calm them. They start
talking about their teachers more quietly, then my
mother comes downstairs and I'm off duty.

I slip past her and up to my room.

I open the letter.

Dear Gwendolyn,
By now you've probably heard that you have a
new schoolmate. He's new in town and visiting
me at The Float Boat tonight. Please come by
and meet him at 7:00 p.m.
Your Faithful Mentor,
Emmeline Forest
P.S. You've met him before.

I stare at this letter from Mrs. Forest, baffled. I
reread it a few times. Who have I met before? No
one. I don't know any boys I haven't grown up with.

It's a mystery.

At dinner, my mother begs me to stop fiddling
with my spaghetti.

"What did Mrs. Forest want?" she asks. She must
have been here when the letter arrived.

"She wants me to meet someone tonight at The Float Boat. They're new in town."

My mother raises an eyebrow. "Meet someone new? How mysterious!" She's right to be surprised. New people don't turn up in Bass Creek all that often. She adds, "You know, there's a new mechanic shop around the corner from The Float Boat. It just opened last week. I noticed a few teenagers out front."

Mechanic? The word rings in my head like it should mean something, but it doesn't.

After clearing up the dinner dishes, I head out into the cool September evening. I stride down the street toward The Float Boat and the Mystery Person. I'm lost in thought (who is it?) when I hear bottles rattling in a shopping cart. The familiar sound comes from a side street, so I stop and wait.

It's Mr. McGillies. His long coat is as filthy as ever, and his thick glasses look exactly like the bottom of one of the bottles that he collects around town in his old grocery cart. He stops his cart in front of me.

"Hi, Mr. McGillies," I say politely. Even though I've been floating above the cornfield and watching his cabin all summer, I haven't seen him for a while and he looks thin and old, more bent over than usual. He almost never looks people in the eye, but this time he does. He looks up at me (he's very short), and his eyes look gigantic behind their glasses. He looks smaller than I remember, like he's drying up and shrivelling. But then, I'm growing.

"Missy has a new friend in town," he says. Mr. McGillies is cryptic at the best of times.

"No, I don't. What do you mean, Mr. McGillies?" I ask. He knows. He knows what's going on at The Float Boat, he knows who I'm meeting. He and Mrs. Forest are totally in on this together. My Watcher and my Mentor, tormenting me for fun.

He grins then starts coughing. I don't remember Mr. McGillies coughing before. When he catches his breath, he slowly rattles away down the sidewalk. Even his rattling seems different from the last time I saw him, slower and quieter.

"Don't fly away now, missy!" he calls softly over his shoulder.

"Thank you, Mr. McGillies." He never says much, it's true, but he has been a good Watcher. Last summer he saved me from the terror of the Shade with just a bottle in his hand. Maybe you don't have to talk much to keep an eye out for people. I think about last night in the laneway outside his cabin …

… *Gwendolyn* …

I shudder and then head on down the street.

FIVE

Mrs. Forest waits for me on the porch of The Float Boat. Candied air wafts out the open door into the darkness, and the warmly lit windows glow.

"Gwendolyn!" she calls. I swing up onto the porch, and Mrs. Forest wraps me in a warm hug, which I allow. It would be impossible to stop her anyway — she's everywhere. My Mentor. I've missed her. We haven't talked much all summer.

"So, who's the Mystery Person?" I ask as I follow her into the store. I feel a little guilty for not talking to Mrs. Forest for weeks, but she doesn't seem to notice. There's no point in feeling guilty, though. It's not easy to be upset in The Float Boat. It's hard to be sour in a candy store.

I step inside, and the Mystery Person grins from the counter.

"Hi, Gwendolyn Golden," he says in a teasing voice.

The Mystery Person has grown since I last saw him. He's unnervingly tall and handsome. How does that happen in a matter of a few months?

"Hi, Everton Miles." My hand goes to my necklace, and I grasp my father's golden feather there. A bad habit when I'm nervous. This is the new boy in town? Everton Miles. I don't know him well. I've only met him once before. But how could I forget him? I remember everything else about that night perfectly, the Midsummer Party. The other Night Flyers. The Spirit Flyers. The singing. Frankly, a night of flying and dancing among old-growth trees with a group of starshot immortals would be a hard thing for anyone to forget.

He's all shoulders and broad chest, long arms and legs, and I know immediately that he's both much wiser and cooler than me, although he's not much older. He has unnervingly dark blue eyes.

Mrs. Forest watches us.

"Remember Everton and his brother Emerson from last summer? At the Night Flyer Midsummer party? They just moved here. Emerson opened a mechanic shop around the corner," she says.

"Yes, I remember. My mom mentioned something about a new mechanic shop," I say.

My, but he is charming. All dark hair, blue eyes, and red lips. His black T-shirt clings nicely to his shoulders. I try hard not to notice.

Mrs. Forest slides into a booth, and I slide in beside her. Everton crams himself into the booth facing us, and for a moment our knees touch under the table. I shoot mine off to the side. Mr. Forest sits one booth over, quietly reading a newspaper. He smiles at me and then goes back to reading.

"Everton is from the city. He's never lived in a small town, Gwen," Mrs. Forest goes on. "Everything is new to him and probably quite strange."

"My old school had five thousand kids," Everton adds. "It wasn't exactly a paragon of virtue or scholarly learning, either."

"What do you mean?" I ask.

"There was a lot of fighting. Drinking. Drugs. Stuff like that. Pretty much what you'd expect."

I want to tell him that I have no expectations of what a city high school might be like, but he keeps talking.

"I wasn't the best student either, to be honest. Hopefully grade ten will be better. What about you? Are you a good student?"

"Good enough, I guess." I shrug. It's a lie; I'm a crap student. But I'm relieved, too. At least he's not going to be popping up in any of my classes.

"Everton's offered to practice your flying skills with you," Mrs. Forest says. "Maybe you can help him adjust to small-town life in return? He can answer questions about being a Night Flyer, and help you with your *choice* next summer."

Choice. Yes, *that* choice, the one that has to be made at the Midsummer Party next year. About who I am and what I'm going to do with my gift. Fly. Not fly. I haven't thought much about it for a while. I've been blocking it out.

"Okay." I'm not at all sure I want flying lessons from Everton Miles. I'm going to feel like his hopeless little sister. I still have trouble with landings.

Mrs. Forest reaches into a bag on the floor and pulls out an enormous book. A little groan escapes me when I see the title: *Your First Flight: A Night Flyer's Handbook*. There's a gold star stamped on the cover that says: *The Complete & Unabridged Version (Newly Updated!)*. The rest of the cover is very familiar. It's a quaint watercolour painting of a mother, father, and young son from the 1950s on the sidewalk dressed in their Sunday best. They're perfectly average-looking, except they're all shoulder-height off the ground.

They're a family of happy Night Flyers.

It's exactly the same cover as the book under my bed, which is not a book. It's actually a box. It's got photos of my dad in it and my golden feather. It's also got my torn and taped three-page brochure, *Your Life as a Night Flyer Starts Today: Your Ten Most Pressing Questions Answered (Micro-Edition for the Less-Than-Willing Reader)*.

Mrs. Forest shoves the gigantic book at me, and I leave it on the table between us. I get it. No more three-page, micro-edition brochure for me.

"Not much of a reader?" Everton asks, amused.

"It's a pretty big book," I answer honestly.

Mrs. Forest brings us tea and we talk a little more about school, and then it's time to go. I drop the *Night Flyer's Handbook* into my backpack and head out into the darkness. The enormous book feels like a block of cement at my back.

As the door closes behind me, I realize I could talk to Mrs. Forest about the winged creature whispering my name. If not Jez, then why not her? She's my Mentor. But there's that stubborn secrecy again. It was late, I was tired, who knows what I saw? It was probably nothing. Right?

Gwendolyn.

SIX

A large set of shoulders jostles me on the sidewalk.

"So what is there to do at night?" Everton asks. He follows me out of The Float Boat so silently, I startle.

"Nothing."

My town closes up after dark. It's not the most exciting place on the planet. A light switches on in the top floor of a house down the street. Everton grins, and not a totally good grin, to be honest. It's a Cheshire Cat grin: Bad Boy Alert.

He jogs then lifts off. His feet rise slowly above my head. He hangs lazily in the air, floating down the sidewalk. This is odd. I've never had a conversation with someone bobbing ahead of me like a balloon. I can suddenly see why Jez always acts a little uneasy when I do it to her. Everton clearly has the hang of flying. I still have to think hard about it most of the time.

"Hey, watch this," he grins. The Bad Boy Alert siren ramps up to three alarms. When either my little brother or sister say, "Hey, watch this," it usually ends in a trip to the hospital. With stitches.

Everton zips to the top of the house with the light on. There's a glow behind the curtains. He peeks in the window then whispers, "They're watching television!" He takes a huge breath then lets out an unholy crowing sound like a rooster. He zips back down to my side and yells, "Run!"

I run. A split second too late. I'm so astonished that I stand and watch the curtains shake and the window fly open. A lady peers down at me. I can't place her, but she's familiar. Then my feet decide to get me out of there and I catch up with Everton.

"That was stupid," I spit at him when we're around the corner.

He grins. "Who cares? She doesn't know who I am."

"She probably knows who I am, though! Thanks a lot. This is a small town, Everton. You better get that through your head."

Everton shrugs and seems pleased with himself.

"I'm leaving," I say and march onto the main street. He catches up to me. "Sorry, Gwendolyn. You're right. I don't know this town, and you do." He's so sincere and there's the full-watt charm beaming at me, too.

"Want to meet my brother?" He grins. He points to a sign behind me: Miles Motors.

"Please?" He looks so goofy and harmless that I roll my eyes and follow him through the big double doors.

It's a big garage filled with tools, boxes, and car parts. It already looks lived-in and comfortable and smells of cars and oily rags. Come to think of it, there was a mechanic shop here before, but I can't remember what it was called or who ran it. I don't drive yet, and I don't think Mom ever brought her car here. A man in overalls looks up at a car raised high on a metal table. He hears us enter.

"Hi!" he calls and walks over. "Gwendolyn Golden, so nice to meet you again. I'm Emerson Miles. Remember us?" He wipes his big greasy hands on a rag. He looks like Everton, except instead of charming he just looks pleasant. His blue eyes twinkle, and his enormous hand engulfs mine as we shake. He's quite a bit older than his little brother.

"Of course, from the Midsummer Party. Welcome to Bass Creek," I say, as welcoming as I can. What I really want to say is, "Why on earth would anyone want to leave the big city to live here?"

"Thanks." Emerson is a Night Flyer too, just like his little brother, except he's kind of a Night Flyer community leader, like Mrs. Forest.

I realize that there are now four Night Flyers in Bass Creek.

It used to be just Mrs. Forest and me, but now with the Miles brothers, we've doubled our numbers overnight. We're becoming almost ordinary, the Night Flyers in this town.

SEVEN

I'm flying.

Night creatures buzz around me. Cornfields wave in the September night below my feet.

Earlier, I walked home from Miles Motors (Everton politely accompanied me at his brother's suggestion), I talked to Mom, I went to bed. I stuffed the copy of *Your First Flight: A Night Flyer's Handbook* (*The Complete & Unabridged Version, Newly Updated!*) under my bed beside the fake box version. Then, hours later when the house was asleep, I flew out my window.

I probably shouldn't have. But I did.

A light breeze moves my hair and brushes my cheek. The dirt road below me is empty, and I try not to glance at the spot where the doll may or may not have been. I ignore the strange flutterings all around me — or is that my heart? I float high enough to see over the cornfield to the distant trees. Mr. McGillies's cabin stands all alone in the darkness next to the forest.

It feels so good to stretch and roll in the air. I drift. I hover. I do a gentle figure eight.

I watch.

A light is on in the cabin again. Mr. McGillies moves back and forth in front of the window. His shadow flickers past, again and again. Why is he still awake?

Suddenly, a shiver of cornstalks rattle below me. A flutter of wings.

My heart hammers.

Gwendolyn.

Then a creature steps out of the field and onto the road below me.

For a second I see him clearly.

A man.

A man with wings. Dark, feathered wings, and a hint of golden eyes, fiery and dangerous-looking.

Gwendolyn.

The whisper comes again. I'm too astonished to move. We really do freeze with terror. Then he's gone in a streak of dark smoke into the stars above. I watch him go, but it's really just a thought, a possibility. There may have been nothing there at all.

I float down to where he stood, and it's suddenly very clear to me that I cannot touch down on this spot. The road where the creature stood is burned and gently smoking.

A black feather rests in the creature's footprint.

I'm horrified as I slowly reach down, although I know this is stupid, stupid, stupid.

Something is making me reach out to the feather. Then at the last moment I snatch my hand away and grasp my father's golden feather around my neck instead. As I watch, the black feather catches fire and burns to ash before my eyes.

"Gwendolyn Golden, fancy meeting you here," a voice says quietly. I start and look up just as Everton Miles steps out of the corn.

EIGHT

Everton walks over to the spot where the black feather just burned to nothing. He pushes the dirt around with his shoe.

"What are you staring at?" he asks.

"Nothing." I stand up straight. "What are *you* doing here?"

"I could ask you the same question. Do you think you should be out here at this hour?" He's teasing me, but there's an edge to his voice. A part of me, a big part, a sensible part, thinks *just tell him what you saw*. But another part, the cowardly sneaky part, holds back. First Jez, then Mrs. Forest, now Everton Miles. I'm a liar, a teller of partial truths.

"I come to this part of the cornfield almost every night. I keep wondering why Mr. McGillies has his light on," I say.

"Oh, yeah, Mr. McGillies is your Watcher." Everton has already steered me away from the spot where the feather burned. He lifts off gently, and I follow.

"Do you know him?" I ask.

Everton shakes his head. "Not really. He likes bottles, I hear." Everton picks up speed. I struggle to keep up.

"You still haven't told me why you're here," I say. We're past the cornfield now, and I can see the houses on the last street in town just ahead, but he doesn't answer me.

We reach the last house then fly silently over the town, over the buzzing streetlights, over the library, over the schoolyard, and back to my house. Everton watches as I float into my bedroom through the window. As soon as I'm inside, he says, "Promise you won't fly out there alone again?"

"Why, Everton? What's out there? And you still haven't told me what you were doing there."

He leans against the window frame and looks at me seriously for a moment.

"It's not safe for you to be out there alone. Come and get me next time if you want to go." Then he's gone.

I watch him vanish into the darkness, and I want to shout *Why? Why isn't it safe out there?* Clearly, Everton Miles knows something I don't. Also, I could point out that he was out there alone, too.

But … I could be wrong. As he fades into the darkness there's a shimmer above him, a flurry and shake of feathers.

They're pure white feathers, with a hint of gold.

NINE

My alarm goes off about thirty seconds later, and I somehow get up for day two of high school. I sneak a strong cup of coffee after Mom and the twins leave, so my heart hammers along, jittery.

Mrs. Mayhew loudly interrogates a boy who cheerfully answers her questions. So far, only Jeffrey Parks has cried. This boy really doesn't seem like the crying type.

"And *Sebastian*, what did you do all summer?" Sebastian starts to tell the class about working on his family's farm. We're getting used to Mrs. Mayhew and her twenty questions. Despite ourselves, we *are* getting to know each other better. The bell rings, and Jez and I jostle down the crowded hallway. I have to find the science room.

"I have to tell you something." I lower my voice. "Mrs. Forest invited me to The Float Boat last night. To meet someone."

Jez perks up. "How mysterious. Who?" I swear her eyes gleam. A few boys look her way, but she doesn't seem to notice.

"A boy. He's new here." I don't have to say anything else. "Him." I point. Everton Miles leans against a locker and talks to a bunch of football players like he grew up in Bass Creek, like he's known them all his life. He's wearing jeans, a little too low for school rules, and a black T-shirt. He also wears a smile that makes it impossible to look away.

Charm just shoots out from him in rays, like beams of light. It even works on adolescent high school football players. Our eyes lock, and he twists up the corner of one perfect red lip at me. Then he goes back to charming the football players. I can't tear my eyes away from him, though. I have no choice.

Not only is Everton Miles slouching against a locker talking to the high school football players like he's their king, but his arm is around a girl.

Everton Miles has his arm around Shelley Norman.

I storm away, flustered. I bang into a few kids who look at me like I'm crazy. Jez runs up behind me and whirls me around. The bell rings for class so we can't talk long.

"Who's that guy? Why do you even know him?"

"That's Everton Miles."

At that very moment, Shelley and Everton snake past down the hall, locked together by Everton's arm.

"I met him last summer at the *party* in the *woods*," I whisper.

"What? Oh," Jez breathes, catching on. "*That* party. Well whoever he is, he's got terrible taste in girls." I could hug Jez sometimes.

"He and his brother just moved here. Mrs. Forest wants him to *help* me ... *you know*." I look up at the ceiling. I can't bring myself to say the word *fly* in the hallway.

"That *is* a secret you might want to keep." She nods. I get a shock of guilt. This is my best friend, and I am keeping a much bigger secret from her.

Gwendolyn.

"Talk to you after school," I say, then run to science class.

I'm late. I walk into the class and fight panic. In high school science you sit at lab tables. With a partner. Two stools per table. Why didn't someone tell me this? Not smart to come to the first science class that requires partners even a second too late.

"Welcome," the teacher says to me, not unkindly. His name is written on the board: Mr. Tupperman. "Please choose a seat."

There are exactly three stools left. Two empty stools are at the Lab Table of the Damned, because it's right at the front of the class. The third empty stool is comfortably midroom, but the stool next to it is already occupied.

Who is sitting there? Martin Evells.

He smiles and raises his hand.

I close my eyes. If I sit at the front of the class all alone at the Lab Table of the Damned, I'll have to help the teacher at every experiment. I'll be his partner in every lab, because I'll be the only person in the classroom sitting alone. Eventually we'll become chummy; I'll clean the boards and empty the beakers after class. I'll call him Mr. T.

I see all this in a second, and then I dash to the empty stool beside Martin Evells. I slide in beside him and drop my books on the desk. I try not to look over at him, but it's no use. I peek, and he smiles at me then looks back up at the teacher.

Don't ask me what else happens in this first day of science class, because I have no idea. There's so much between me and the boy I'm sitting beside, although we're just a few inches apart. Best friends long ago, a terrible mother who starts rumours about me, the Worst Kiss Ever.

But more than all that (and I could write a book about why), Martin Evells knows that I can fly.

TEN

Day two of high school finally ends.

I walk toward the front doors of the school to wait for Jez when Miss Moreau walks past me. She stops and does a double-take. I can't avoid her, so I stand still as she draws up close and peers into my face. Everyone else pushes past us to go outside. I think of a rock in the river, stalling the salmon migration.

"Miss Moreau?" I finally say, because she's really staring at me.

"It WAS you," she says. "Last night. Someone did a rooster impression outside my bedroom window. It was you." She stands back, sure of herself now, and crosses her arms. She's got a slightly friendly look on her face, though, the kind of look an adult gives you when they know they're right. And they've got you. Of course it was her! I knew I recognized the surprised face in the window. My heart sinks.

"Actually, Miss Moreau, I was there, yes, but that wasn't me. Doing the roostering. Not me." I shake my head, wondering if *roostering* is a word.

She raises her eyebrow. "Well, whoever it was, they're really loud. They sounded like they were right outside my window, which would be difficult since it's three storeys up."

"Yes, difficult. Impossible, really," I say, weakly.

She's about to say more when Mr. Skinty walks up and says, "Gwendolyn Golden?" Miss Moreau and I look at him in surprise, and I nod. The hallway is empty now. Everyone is out on the front lawn in the September sunshine. This is good, since it looks like I'm in trouble, caught between the principal and a teacher. I don't need the whole school watching.

"Miss Golden, please come with me."

Miss Moreau walks away, so maybe I'm off the hook.

I follow Mr. Stinky ... Skinty! Skinty! ... down the hall. He slouches. I almost want to tell him to straighten up. He doesn't say a word, so I just follow him. What can this possibly be about?

"Through here, Miss Golden."

I walk into his office and there, sitting like two damaged little angels, are my brother and sister. Christopher has a tissue stuffed up against a bloody nose. His shirt is torn at the sleeve, and his hair is all over the place. Christine has a bandage on one cheek and an ice pack on her hand.

They're a mess.

I've been in charge of C2 since they were born. Plenty of times I've had to haul them off each other or discipline them or sort out something with their teachers. I've walked them home every day since they were in nursery school, and technically speaking, they should be in school right now, since their day isn't over yet. In fact, I should be meeting them on the front steps in about fifteen minutes. I've never been this unnerved before.

But something about these two seven-year-olds, all banged up and staring at me from the over-stuffed chairs in my new principal's office, something about them just makes my knees weak. It's only the second day of school. What happened?

I sit down and shoot C2 a sympathetic look.

"What's going on?" I ask Mr. Skinty. He sits in the leather chair behind a large wooden desk, which looks like an ocean between us.

"Your brother and sister have been fighting. Not with each other," he says. "They were causing havoc, it seems, so their principal, Mrs. Abernathy, has kindly dropped them off here." He raises his eyebrows at me in a "they're-your-problem-now" look.

"Where's our mom?" I ask.

"Mrs. Abernathy couldn't reach her, and it was very important, urgent in fact, that they be removed from the school premises."

I look over at C2, the Chrissies, and my heart breaks a little. What on earth did they do? My little brother looks like he'd like to cry but won't, although he's the gentler of the two. My little sister, though, she's all spit and vinegar and fight. Like a tiny wounded tiger.

She glares at me, but Christopher's eyes are soft and full of tears.

I take a deep breath. What would my mom say if she were here? Or Mrs. Forest?

"Okay. Um, maybe they should tell us what happened?" I try to be diplomatic, but Mr. Skinty breaks in.

"It's not really important at the moment. Mrs. Abernathy will report the incident — incidents — to your mother as soon as she can reach her. We really just needed a family member to take responsibility for them before the school day was out. You can take them now."

Then I swear, that man just gets up and walks out.

I'm shocked. I watch him go, my mouth open. Mrs. Abernathy is always so motherly, so concerned for our welfare. Not this principal.

I look back at my brother and sister. Christopher succumbs to his tears and uses his blood-covered tissue to wipe his eyes. I reach across the principal's desk and hand him a new, clean one, which he takes with a sniffle. My sister, though, oh, my sister.

She screws up her eyes and yells at the top of her angry, spitfire lungs, "You're not Mr. Skinty! You're MR. STINKY!"

ELEVEN

I gather up C2 and get them out of there. No one seems to notice. Even the lady at the front desk ignores us. Clearly I'm taking two upset young kids out of the principal's office, but she doesn't look up from her computer.

Maybe someone died! I think. *Maybe our house has burned to the ground and taken all our belongings, and pets, and birthday presents!*

I glare at the lady as we walk by, but she doesn't notice.

Christopher takes my hand and is gently hiccupping as we walk out the school front door. Christine trails behind us, mumbling and darting dark looks everywhere. She drags her backpack along the floor and bump-bumps it down the front stairs of the school in protest. Outside I get her to wear her backpack, then I take them both by the hand and we head home. Everyone is gone, so there's no one to watch me and my angry, bleeding siblings slink down the sidewalk.

As gently as I can, I begin to prod them about what happened. The story comes out in slow, irregular drips like a leaky tap. There's plenty of waiting between drips.

"So," I say as we walk along, "were you mad at someone?"

Drip.

"David Plummer." This is Christine.

Drip.

"David Plummer? What a crap name! David Dumber is more like it." I've learned that teasing is a great way to loosen them up, but you have to be careful not to overdo it. Teasing can so easily lurch into taunting.

Drip … d … d … drip.

"I hate him." Christine wipes an angry tear off the end of her nose.

"Yes?" Agreeing helps and often opens the faucet to faster drips.

"I think he's retarded."

"Retarded? Really? Do you know what that means?"

Drip … drip … drip …

Christine plants her feet and sticks her hands on her hips. She stomps one foot. Here comes the flood.

"It's just that he's SO STUPID! And he sits beside me! And he's always in the way! And he never gets the right answer, never, and he … he … and he told me that our dad disappeared because he didn't love us!" Christine turns into a puddle of distress on the sidewalk right in front of me, and all I can do is put my arm around her shoulder and let her broken faucet wash over us.

After she calms down a bit, I say things like David Dumber is dead wrong. No one gets to talk about Dad like that. I knew him, and you didn't. He really did love us, more than anything. We had nothing to do with his disappearance.

His death.

As I murmur comforting things to Christine and we begin to walk again, I finally understand the term *heartsick*. How can a seven-year-old say something like that to another child? I know that our family is a little strange, different, even scary for some people maybe, what with a disappearing dad and an angry, possibly drug-addicted older child like me. Let's not even mention the flying around at night part (which is something C2 don't know about me anyway. Mom and I decided to keep it from them for now). But as for my vanishing father, can't the world just leave my little brother and sister out of it?

David Plummer didn't think up something that mean by himself, so his parents must say that about our family at home. He heard it from them. Is that what people say about my family behind our backs? That Dad left because he didn't love us? Not that he died?

I realize with a start that I was almost the same age Christine and Christopher are now when my father disappeared. I must have looked a lot like Christine does, all banged up and sad, although she has way more fire in her than I ever did. She's so little! I get an ache so deep that I want to burst into tears too, but I can't, not in front of C2.

I can take the rumours and loneliness, but *no one* gets to hurt them. I'm going to have to raise up my shield, throw whatever protective charm I can over them. I should be able to figure out how to do that. Maybe just up the crazy ante, start flying around in public so no one gives C2 a second thought. All eyes would be firmly on me, not on them.

But it would never work. We're all in this together.

Christine quiets and slowly walks behind us. I turn to my little brother, who has held my hand all the way and is strangely quiet.

"So do you want to tell us about your angry day?" I try to sound breezy and bright, but Christopher keeps a stony silence. His faucet isn't leaky.

"Did you meet up with a nasty kid? A dumb quiet-time story? A rotten carrot stick at snack-time?"

Christopher clenches his jaw, which I've never seen him do before. "Does David Plummer have black hair?" he asks his sister. She nods.

"Why do you want to know what David Dumber looks like?" I ask, trying to keep it light. My little brother looks up at me, the sweet one, the kind one, the first to laugh or cry.

"I'm going to fight him. I'm going to fight David Plummer." I'm so shocked that I gasp.

"*What?*"

Christine skips up, happier now.

"You heard him. He's gonna fight Dumb David Dumber."

It's like watching two kids from a horror movie. The twins are suddenly happier. They perk up and walk ahead of me down the sidewalk, chattering away like nothing just happened. I'm in way over my head here. Christopher never fights. Never, not even with his twin. Not really. He just gives in. Two days separated at school, and he's already talking about fighting other kids?

I really, really hope our mother is home when we get there.

TWELVE

When we get home, Cassie waddles up to us, wagging her stubby tail. C2 tear toward the kitchen, and I see our mother in the living room. Mrs. Abernathy is sitting beside her.

This has never happened before.

A school official has never visited our home. Police officers on account of me, yes. But up until this moment, we've never had an official visit from the principal.

Christopher and Christine skid to a halt and stare. Christine is the first to look a little worried. Her face gets stormy, and I can see that the faucet could burst again.

I step up.

"Hi, Mrs. Abernathy. I'll make a snack for everyone."

My mother says, "Thank you, Gwen." Then the adults turn back to their conversation. I lead C2 into the kitchen and make them crackers and cheese. I pour two glasses of milk.

"Are we in trouble?" Christine whispers.

"Of course you're in trouble. I'm going to talk to them. Don't move out of these seats," I say, serious. I still have some sway with them. Enough to make them stay in the kitchen for a few moments, anyway. I head into the living room.

Mrs. Abernathy says kindly, "Your brother and sister had a very bad day, I'm afraid, Gwendolyn. Your sister argued with a boy rather loudly. He's quite unnerved."

"David Plummer," I say.

"Yes. And your little brother threw a tantrum and spat on his teacher because she asked him to sit down." I'm shocked. The thought of my little brother spitting on an adult is impossible.

"Are you sure?" I ask. "He *spat* on her?"

Mrs. Abernathy nods. "I'm afraid so." She looks a little stricken, too. She knows us all well.

"Maybe we should move them back into the same class, and this behaviour will stop?" my mother says. She's got a hopeful tone to her voice that hurts to hear. A pleading mother.

"They've never been apart before," I add.

What I don't say: *However, there's the small fact that my brother just told me he was going to fight someone.*

Mrs. Abernathy is kind. She nods but somehow shakes her head at the same time, agreeing and disagreeing at once.

"I know why you think that, but don't you see? Christine and Christopher absolutely have to learn how to be apart. How are they going to grow up if they can't be separated, even for a small part of the day?" She makes a lot sense. I hate it, but I can't argue with her.

She goes on, "The school board psychologist thinks the twins would benefit from play-based family therapy. There's a new therapist in town who's good with children and adolescents. His name is Adam Parks. Christine and Christopher can go together. It's got amazing potential to help them sort out their identity issues."

My mother sighs and takes a sip of her tea.

A small movement catches the corner of my eye, and I see my little sister's pink running shoe zip back into the kitchen. *Busted. Christine, you are never going to follow the rules.*

I love that about you.

THIRTEEN

After Mrs. Abernathy leaves, the rest of the evening is normal enough. C2 seem to be perfectly happy and content. They chatter away through dinner, they do their homework, they play with Cassie. Normal.

Once I'm alone in my room, I think about last night. I see a black feather, Everton walking out of the corn, a flutter of white feathers.

Gwendolyn.

It's time. I reach under the bed and pull out *Your First Flight: A Night Flyer's Handbook (The Complete & Unabridged Version, Newly Updated!).* I fan through hundreds of pages. It looks so dull that I feel a little headachy. Fortunately, there are lots of drawings and photographs. I should search the index at the back for "dark winged creature, burning feather."

That would be wise. But I don't. If I don't know anything about it, then maybe it's not really there. Instead, I flip through the chapters then stop near the beginning of *Chapter One: History and Hysteria.*

The illustrations are horrifying. They're all inky, darkness and light.

The first drawing takes up a whole page and it's titled, "*Misfortunes of the Night Flying Monster, 1447.*" It's drawn by someone named "T. Bosch." It's a work of misery and fear, but I can't look away.

A young woman in chains walks along a dark stormy road in the summer. She's wearing a long, old-fashioned skirt, a loose white shirt, and her hair blows around her. A group of angry, shouting men hold pitchforks at her back and prod her along.

Misfortunes of the Night Flying Monster.

I switch my desk light on and study the picture with my nose right up to the book. The men look like farmers, like men who know how to use a pitchfork. The woman, the Night Flyer, the *monster*, is young. Very young. My age, maybe. In fact, she looks a *lot* like me. The pitchforks jab at her, tearing her long skirt. She looks fearful, but T. Bosch catches something else on her face, too. She's not crying. Hers is the only face looking right out at whoever looks at the picture. She stares right at me. Her chin is up, her head is back, her jaw is set.

Determined. That's the look. Like she's saying, "Jab away all you want, I know who I am." I read a little of the page:

… from the fifteenth-century records of the first use of the term "Night Flyer." There appears to have been spirited rejection of the medieval European Night Flyer population, and as Professor Gertrude L. Lisquith (N.F., Ph.D, Oxford), concludes in her lengthy and definitive 1963

study, The Dialectic Presented by the Earliest Records of Night Flying/Non-Witch Identified Populations in Medieval England, France, Germany and Belgium, *(Oxford University Press, pp. 816–865), although Night Flyers most likely existed before 1437, we have virtually no written record of them. More study must be made of oral/pre-literary traditions and cultural references to Night Flying individuals or family populations in medieval Europe.*

I force myself to get to the end of this paragraph. It's not easy. I think of my taped and torn three-page micro-edition brochure for the Less-Than-Willing-Reader in the box-book beneath my bed. Life was so simple just a few short months ago. But frankly, the picture of *Misfortunes of the Night Flying Monster* pretty much says it all. Pitchforks. A dark road. Angry men. A girl in chains. *Monster.* You don't have to be Professor Gertrude L. Lisquith (N.F., Ph.D, Oxford) to get it.

A few more flips through the pages, and there's another T. Bosch ink drawing. This one stops me cold. It's titled, *The Monster Meets Her End, 1449.*

This time the same young woman is falling, falling through the sky. She's whirling in a downward spiral, her head flung back, her mouth open in a scream and her arms above her head, her skirt and long hair blowing upward. Dark clouds form around her, and demons pop out from the clouds as she plummets past. The demons have pitchforks in their hands. What's with all the farm implements? I look closer. There, at the top of the image, hidden among the swirls of the night sky, is a darker cloud. I gasp. I draw my nose right up to the picture and squint. I wish I had a magnifying glass.

It's a darker cloud, alright. And there are eyes in it. And teeth and fingernails. A toe plainly sticks out at one end of the cloud. There's no doubt about it: T. Bosch has seen the *Shade*, the unspeakable darkness that chased me from the sky and almost killed me last spring. This image, this plummeting girl, was very nearly me. If not for Mr. McGillies fighting off the Shade with his bottles, I might have been the monster who met her end.

But he saved me from the Shade.

My heart starts to beat painfully in my chest, and that bad night with the Shade comes right back at me, the teeth, the fingernails, the toes, the voices all screaming and crying my name....

... my door pops open, and I jump up and knock the chair over.

"Good heavens, Gwendolyn, whatever you're reading, put it away right now and go to bed. Goodnight!"

"Goodnight, Mom," I whisper, not looking up. My door closes. As soon as she's gone, I flip to the index at the back of the book and look up "feathered man." There's an entry on page 787 near the end of the book in a chapter titled, "Enemies and Entities."

My hands tremble as I flip to the page, and there he is, the dark wings, the dark body, the smoky face and hair, the golden eyes, all the same. It's another illustration by T. Bosch, and the feathered man is walking along the same road from the earlier illustrations, but no one is around this time. The caption reads, "Rogue Spirit Flyer *Abilith*, as described to T. Bosch, 1452."

The creature has a name. Abilith.

I read on.

Rogue Spirit Flyer (RSF): extremely rare, probably mythical or nonexistent. RSF are said to be immortal and are technically a fallen or defiled Spirit Flyer. The idea that the 'Rogue will get you' is a story Night Flying parents have told their children to keep them from wandering into danger and dates back to the earliest Night Flyer legends. Bellamy D. Clementine (Ph.D, Sometime Reader of Divinity, Cambridge) notes that the first written evidence of RSFs is in the Geronima Parchment, ca. 1445. The RSF is said to carry a shoulder of heavy black feathers and preys upon the weak and unsuspecting, in lonely, out of the way places. He is beguiling, clever, handsome of face and limb, well-spoken, and dangerous. He is alone, shunned, a miscreant and blackguard. Light and truth do not follow him; fire and malice do. He abandons the ways of humans and non-humans alike to live separate and apart in all things. For this reason, he will never enter a town or well-inhabited village or hamlet and will often shun even two people together. The few unsubstantiated stories that have existed through the centuries suggest that rather than live for all eternity alone, occasionally an RSF will choose a Night Flyer for a companion and beguile that person into believing him or herself a fellow RSF.

The Legend of Abilith and Mirandel, ca. 1440: *One very early (and again unsubstantiated) medieval* *legend tells of Mirandel, a young Night Flyer, who was stolen away by the Rogue Abilith. He was said to whisper her name, leave her gifts, and upon touching one, she vanished forever. His gifts included glass beads, cornstalk dolls, and burning feathers. For further reading, see also this book:* Old Wives Tales, Fairy Tales, and Legends.

I slam the book shut. I break into a sweat and my heart actually hurts, it pounds so hard against my ribcage.

There's a legendary Rogue Spirit Flyer in the cornfield outside Mr. McGillies's cabin.

He's left me gifts, twice now. A doll with glass beads for eyes, a burning feather.

I've seen him. And he's calling my name.

FOURTEEN

It's Friday morning. *Your First Flight: A Night Flyer's Handbook (The Complete & Unabridged Version, Newly Updated!)* is hidden under my bed beneath a pile of laundry. I'm not looking at it again, maybe never. I've decided it's more important than ever not to mention the fact that I may have seen a Rogue Spirit Flyer to anyone, not Everton, not Mrs. Forest, especially not Jez. It's *legendary* and *extremely rare*, according to the handbook. And very unlikely that I actually saw it.

Deny, deny, deny.

Instead, for the rest of the first week of high school, I go to bed early and wake up every morning and go to class like any normal teenager. Simple, mindless activity is good.

There's nothing more mindless than pottery class. I sit on a bench beside Jez, who talked me into this. She said pottery class would be easy and fun. I needed one grade nine art credit, and now I'm about to stick my hands in a lump of swirling clay.

The teacher, a middle-aged man with a grey ponytail who wants us to call him "Chas" (although his name is "Charles," and what would be wrong with calling him "Mr. Whatever-His-Last-Name-Is?"), has been over-helpful with us.

It's been hard not to roll my eyes.

As soon as we walk into the room, we have a "creation smock ceremony." Clay-covered smocks hang on the wall, and we're supposed to pick the one that "speaks" to us. The smocks certainly look old enough to talk. According to Chas, each smock holds the "creative energy" of previous grade nine pottery students struggling to create the perfect ashtray or mug.

"Yes, Michael Cherry made a fantastic sculpted horse-head in that last year," Chas says when Jez picks her smock and gingerly puts it on.

I desperately try not to snort. I cannot look at Jez, whose eyes are wide with disbelief. When it's my turn, I grab the cleanest smock I can find and slam it over my head. Chas smiles sweetly and whispers quietly, "Interesting choice, Gwendolyn. That smock belonged to Shelley Norman. A wonderful ashtray-maker, good with mugs, too. She was my best student last year. This is a good start for you." Then Chas moves off to the next student.

I want to tear the smock off over my head and stomp on it. I briefly wonder what Chas will say if I do? I already know that he would respect my "creative choice." He would nod and hmm and whisper, saying that the smock did not speak to me, and he'd ask me to "experience" another smock.

This is what I would have done, but the smocks are all chosen. So I'm stuck with it. I can smell Shelley on it, a little body odour mixed with nastiness. Later in the class, he comes and slaps a handwritten label onto our backs with our initials. Sure enough, he covers "S.N." with my "G.G.," and I'm forever adorned with the smock of mine enemy. And Everton's girlfriend. Shelley Norman is now all around me, literally smothering me.

I spin the pottery table with my right foot, about to form gross wet clay with my hands.

"So how's Everton?" Jez asks quietly. I frown. I dip my hands in the clay-covered margarine tub of water beside me and pick up the clay blob. I plop it into the centre of the spinning table like Chas taught us and start to form it. It's slippery and cool and seriously looks like a pile of poop. I could tell Jez the truth, start at the beginning, mention the winged man, what I found in the *Night Flyer's Handbook* about Rogue Spirit Flyers. Tell her that Everton walked out of the cornfield at the very moment that the Rogue's black feather burned to ash.

Or I could lie.

"I have no idea. I haven't seen him or his girlfriend all week." I can't for some reason say Shelley Norman's name out loud. I suddenly have a vision of the smock coming to life if I breathe its former owner's name. Shelley's clay face would pop out of my chest and whisper something bizarre like, "The darkest clay forms solitary figures at midnight."

Weird thought, but the whole pottery thing is weirding me out.

Jez isn't really listening. She's concentrating on her blob of clay. My own blob is now a lopsided mess. I change the subject.

"So the twins are having identity and anger issues. The school is suggesting therapy."

"Oh! Well, my cousin went to therapy for all of grade three. It made him a lot nicer." But she's not really paying attention to our conversation, because she's busy creating a masterpiece. There before her on the pottery wheel is a perfectly formed clay goblet. Yes, not only is my best friend good at high school, she's also a natural at clay. I love her too much to be jealous.

But it figures. It really does.

Since I'm not telling her the truth about Everton, or about a legendary Rogue Spirit Flyer whispering my name at the edge of town, I can't really complain too much.

FIFTEEN

It's Saturday night, and everyone is asleep. Except me.

All is silent and dark. I'm at my open window, fully dressed, the screen wide on its hinges. I look over our backyard, over the neighbour's fence, into the lane that leads to Jez's street, then off to the edge of the town.

Every piece of me wants to fly out the window.

But there's the small issue of the Rogue Spirit Flyer.

Clearly, I'm going to have to tell someone about this creature. But I really don't want to. It's so unlikely, and I probably imagined it. And honestly, who would believe me? Why would I get to see an extremely unlikely (and *unsubstantiated*) legend? It's like seeing the Loch Ness monster or something.

Maybe I should find out more information, go on a fact-finding mission. That girl in the legend, Mirandel, she disappeared when she touched something the Rogue named Abilith left for her. I'll just be careful not to touch anything. The truth is, the thought of NOT flying out to Mr. McGillies's cabin is torture. I'm dying to fly out into the beautiful night, and I'm angry that I have to be afraid.

For a moment I can hear the Rogue's whisper, the whisper I've been hearing in my head all week, like a silky, gentle rustling of corn and night creatures.

Gwendolyn.

Then a real voice says right in my ear, "Penny for your thoughts."

I almost jump out of my skin, another one of those sayings that is weirdly accurate. Everton hovers off the roof above me.

"What can Gwendolyn Golden be thinking with such a dark look on her face?"

"Everton! How long have you been there? What's wrong with you? You can't just lurk around people's windows!" He flies down level to my window (although still out of reach I notice) and apologizes.

"Sorry, Gwen, you're right. But what *were* you thinking?"

"I'm just, I'm … what do you want, Everton?" He grins like the Cheshire Cat.

"Come on, Gwendolyn, don't you want to show me your town?"

"Why would I want to do that?" But a devious little part of me thinks, *If Everton is with me, I'll feel safer.* He looks at me with dark blue eyes, and I give in. For my own reasons, of course, it has nothing to do with him being charming and persuasive.

"Fine." I slip out of the window and float past him. We're going to the only place that holds any interest for me, with or without a legendary creature calling me. I want to find out more, that's the truth. Plus, the tug to see Mr. McGillies's cabin again is overpowering.

I get a little ahead of him then look over my shoulder. He pokes his head into my bedroom window.

"Hey!" I shout. "Are you a voyeur or something? Get out of my room!" He laughs and flies toward me. My faces blazes a little as I try not to picture the socks and underwear all over my bedroom floor.

We head out. I'm not as good at flying as he is, so I waver and dip, and when I do, he calmly flips onto his back like an expert swimmer treading water, waiting for the weaker swimmer to catch up. There's nothing I can do about this, but it's annoying. I point out buildings to him as we float along and he smiles and nods and says, "Interesting."

We pass the library, which slides below us, and I say like an idiot, "That's the library."

"Interesting," he says for the twelfth time. I float down to land on the roof of the library.

"No, it's not. Nothing about this town is interesting. Why do you keep saying that? I happen to live here. It's really not that bad."

Everton touches down effortlessly beside me. The library roof has little pebbles stuck forever in roofing tar. It's a pretty view down the main street, past all the stores. The Float Boat is just at the edge of my vision. I can see the top of the high school a few streets over.

"You're right, it's a dull town." Everton takes a seat on a chimney and leans back to look at the sky.

The next words just pop out of my mouth.

"So, you're dating Shelley Norman. Nice."

Everton shrugs. "Not really dating per se. That's kind of dramatic, don't you think? But Shelley and I are a lot alike. You don't like her?"

Now it's my turn to shrug. "She's my mortal enemy, okay. She makes dolls that look like me and sticks pins in them. No, I don't like her. And I'm pretty sure it's mutual."

Everton surprises me with a smile. "She doesn't really like anyone, so don't take it personally. She doesn't have the best home life." Then he takes off into the night. I follow. I want to mutter that Shelley Norman deserves a terrible home life, which is a bit dark, even for me. I'm curious, though. What does he mean?

We travel for a while in silence. We float soundlessly over the town, and like every other night, I'm drawn to the cornfields. As the houses thin beneath us, I slip a quick look at Everton. It's obvious I'm taking us back to Mr. McGillies's cabin. When we finally get close, Everton stops and looks quizzically at me.

"Is this your favourite place or something?"

"Sort of. I come here a lot, but you said it was dangerous."

He looks at me slyly. "I said it's dangerous for *you*, and *you* shouldn't go alone. You're not. You're with me." He's not going to tell me more.

We reach the cornfields, and there's Mr. McGillies's cabin. The light is on in the window again. He's still up, and it's one thirty in the morning. Everton floats lazily behind me and catches up when I stop. I just can't cross the field. I'm stuck as though I'm tethered from my ankle to the road.

"Why did you stop?" he asks. He flips onto his back and looks up at the deep velvety sky then grins over at me. It's impossible to describe this feeling of being stuck, so I stay quiet. I look around for black feathers. I strain my ears for any whispering, but all is calm and silent. It's so quiet that we can both hear the CREAK of the front door of the cabin as it opens. A figure steps out, and a small light bumps into the field.

A flashlight?

Everton draws up beside me and whispers, "Aren't you the tiniest bit curious why your Watcher is out in the darkness at one thirty in the morning?" His breath tickles my ear. I *am* curious. I'm burning with curiosity, to be honest. Then the cabin door opens again, and another bouncing light heads for the open field. Two people out in the darkness?

The flashlights flicker up and down. In a second, Everton is over the field, floating toward the cabin, and I can't stop him. I don't want to be left behind either, so I have no choice. I have to fly over the cornfield.

I don't look down. I don't think about the feathered man. I don't think about the Shade or *The Monster Meets Her End, 1449*. Instead I think about the girl being poked along by pitchforks, and her chin jutting up and out, looking straight at me.

I fly as fast as I can to catch up to Everton, but he keeps ahead of me without trying. We're almost across the cornfield and closer to the cabin. The dark trees of the forest come nearer and nearer. I keep my eyes on the bouncing flashlights. Suddenly, voices.

Mr. McGillies. And ... a boy.

Everton lands gently on the roof of the cabin and waves me over. I land as quietly as I can, although I'm still pretty loud. I creep across the roof and lie on my stomach beside him. We peek over the chimney ...

... and see Mr. McGillies standing in the field.

Martin Evells is at his side.

What?

WHAT?

I can't believe what I'm seeing. What earthly reason could bring Martin Evells here at this hour? The world does a flip for a second, and I have to grab the rooftop to steady myself. I suddenly worry I'm going to slip and fall. Everton watches the old man and the boy. I strain to listen.

"Here, Martin?" Mr. McGillies strobes his flashlight across the yard. Something shines out in the darkness as the light flickers over it: an enormous mountain of glass bottles. It must be the largest collection of bottles in the world. It reaches halfway up the cabin wall. But it's possible, since Mr. McGillies has been collecting bottles for as long as I can remember. The effect of the flashlights shining on the bottles is magical. They glimmer and glint like fireflies where the light catches them. It looks like a mountain of treasure glinting in the darkness.

"Yes. Perfect, Mr. McGillies, right here, close to your back window so you can see it. We can start building it tomorrow," Martin answers. Then he moves forward and takes Mr. McGillies by the arm.

"Come back inside," Martin says. He's as tender and caring as any mother with her child. I simply can't fathom this. What is Martin doing here?

And why is he being so sweet to Mr. McGillies?

The two walk below us, and I can't see Mr. McGillies very well, because he's all stooped. But I see Martin's face, and I'm struck by the intensity I see there. And the care. It feels wrong to be watching the two of them like this. I suddenly pray that Martin doesn't look up and see me. They go back into the house, and Everton lifts off the roof.

"We should make the evening more exciting for them, don't you think?" His eyes get wide, and I see what he's going to do.

I launch myself at him, and he hits the roof with a thud, tiles digging into his spine.

"You are NOT going to scream like a rooster outside anyone's window!"

Even I'm scared. This comes out of me in an unholy snarl. I don't care. Everton grunts a little as I shove my knee deep into his stomach, and he wheezes.

"Gwendolyn, you *do* have a temper. A few people said so, but I didn't believe them." He gently pushes my knee off him and sits up. "Okay, I'll leave your Watcher alone. Don't worry."

I'm about to snarl that he better, but the door flies open below us, and Mr. McGillies's shaky old voice shouts into the darkness: "I hear you bumping around on my roof! Be off now, foul thing, you Rogue! There's nothing for your feathers of fire here!"

I freeze.

Rogue? Feathers of fire?

Everton snaps to attention and sits upright. He puts his fingers to his lips in a *shhh* and looks quickly out to the darkness of fields and trees. I hear Martin tell Mr. McGillies to shut the door, and as soon as he does, Everton grabs my arm and we launch into the air at top speed. We zip back over the cornfield.

There's something following us, something travelling as fast as we are.

"Everton, what's behind us?" I shout.

"Don't look back! Fly, Gwendolyn!"

I fly as fast as I can. There are more noises behind us, and I can't help it. I have to know what's going on. I twist my head, and there's a creature hot on our heels.

Pure white feathers flash like the sun.

I gasp and close my eyes tight, then open them. There's nothing behind us. We fly faster than I thought I could. We shriek into town and land on the library roof. Everton collapses onto the pebbles and tar, and I sit down hard beside him.

"What … what was chasing us?" I gasp, trying to catch my breath. I'm about to get even louder when a gentle voice arrives in my head.

Gwendolyn Golden, Everton Miles is protecting you. As am I.

Then I swear, a pure white creature lands gracefully on the library roof beside me. I can't do anything but stare, even though I've seen this kind of creature before. I look from the shimmering figure to Everton. I'm astonished.

Everton says quietly, "Gwendolyn Golden, meet Celestine. My friend, the Spirit Flyer."

SIXTEEN

I stare at Everton, although I do sneak a few peeks at the Spirit Flyer, the starshot immortal of light and air standing nearby. I try not to act too surprised. I've seen her kind before, and I shouldn't gawk, but it's hard not to. Here are the white feathers and the hint of gold I saw the last time Everton flew me home.

The Spirit Flyer is tall, taller than I remember from the Midsummer Party. She, for this Spirit Flyer certainly seems like a girl, and I think Celestine is a girl's name, glows gently in the darkness, but she politely keeps her distance. Everton sits up.

"She's helping me, Gwen."

"Helping you? What are you doing?" Everton doesn't answer, but Celestine's Spirit Flyer voice arrives in my head.

We are seeking the dark Rogue, Gwendolyn Golden.

Everton nods. "Didn't you hear your Watcher? *Be off, foul thing? Rogue? Feathers of fire?* We thought the Rogue existed, but we weren't sure."

A horrible pain forms in the pit of my stomach.

"So there's probably a *Rogue* around Mr. McGillies's shack. A Rogue Spirit Flyer. I've wondered. I've been trying to track it, Celestine and I have been trying to lure it, but it's slippery and smart. You probably don't know what a Rogue is, though." He looks at me and I squirm.

"I've seen it."

Everton stares at me. "What?"

"I've seen it. The Rogue. It called my name from the corn. It left me a corn husk doll and a burning feather. That's what I was looking at the first time you found me there." I see a lot of things cross Everton's face, disbelief, surprise, anger, concern, before he can compose himself and speak.

"You're lucky, Gwendolyn. Stupid and lucky. You have no idea. If you've seen this Rogue, it didn't want you dead. That's the only possible reason you're still alive."

There is another possibility, Everton Miles.

A deep look of worry creases his forehead.

"What?" I demand. "What possibility? Tell me."

"Nothing, it's just a legend."

"No, it's not."

Celestine isn't going to say any more. Everton looks at me a long time. The silence makes me jittery. Then Everton lets out a long breath.

"I'd be really famous if I saw the Rogue. Celestine is the youngest of her kind. She'd gain respect among the other Spirit Flyers if she caught it and took it to her older brothers and sisters. They're always searching for it. But we can't get close to it." He pauses. "It's here for a reason, though. I think it's here for you."

I start to argue, but Celestine speaks in my head again.

Gwendolyn Golden, the Rogue has been solitary for centuries, roaming the dark isolation of space. It is lonely and seeks companionship. But you have accomplished something that we have not, for Everton Miles and I have not seen it. If you have, beware. Everton Miles may be correct. It may have chosen you.

"What? Why? Me? You're wrong!" I'm scared now. Celestine shakes her golden head.

You must be careful, never solitary, Gwendolyn Golden. You are safe in the confines of your village, but you must call Everton and me to you when you travel alone.

"How do I call you?"

You think of me, and I shall come. Go safely, Gwendolyn Golden, until we meet again.

Then Celestine is gone in a gentle golden shimmer. I turn on Everton.

"How exactly did you join forces with a *Spirit Flyer*?" I must sound mad, because Everton looks worried.

"We were around Mr. McGillies's cabin. A lot."

"Why didn't I see you there?" He shakes his head.

"Sorry, Gwendolyn, but you're not very good at not being seen."

Suddenly I'm exhausted, and I stumble on the library roof. Everton catches me and for a moment holds me tight.

"Are you okay, Gwen?" he whispers. I nod and pull away.

"I'm going home," I say and float gently into the night. Everton sticks by my side all the way. I reach my house, open the window latch, and float into my room. He watches me settle on my bed.

"Gwendolyn, a Rogue doesn't like people. Celestine said you're okay in town, or with a friend out of town. But don't go to Mr. McGillies's cabin alone again. You have to promise me." I nod and roll over in my bed.

"Goodnight, Everton," I mumble.

You'd think it would take a person forever to fall asleep after a night like that, but it doesn't. I tumble into weird dreams of a golden Spirit Flyer and a dark-feathered figure, both calling my name. And a charming, dark-haired boy who stands guard by my window all night long.

Everton Miles is a teenage Rogue-hunter with terrible taste in girls and a shimmering, underage Spirit Flyer for a friend.

If I didn't think so before, I do now: it's entirely possible that Everton Miles is stranger than me.

SEVENTEEN

I wake with a start. I've overslept. Sunshine pours in the window, and I have a hard time picturing the events of last night.

Did I really see Martin Evells and Mr. McGillies at the cabin? Did Everton Miles really introduce me to a Spirit Flyer? Is it possible that some fallen, legendary creature is really looking for me?

None of it seems remotely real, and I realize in the interest of my sanity, I have to get outside and do something normal. So, today is the day I'll hand my old paper route to the twins.

Before I do though, I take a quick look through the *Night Flyer's Handbook* for anything about Spirit Flyers. Nothing. Not a word.

Curious.

When I tell C2 over lunch that today's the day they start my paper route, they're ridiculously excited. We trundle the old wagon around with Cassie's leash tied to the handle, and I try not to keep looking up into the autumn sky for dark feathers.

Instead I show my little brother and sister where to find the big bag of flat papers at the corner of our street, how to roll them and stack them into the wagon. Christine holds the list of addresses, and she marches us down the street like a sergeant major.

We get to the first house. Christopher is an amazing shot — he never misses. His sister tells him where to throw the first paper, and he parks it right there. At the first house, he bounces the paper off the door and onto the welcome mat. Then we go to the next house, and the paper lands on the rocking chair. Then at the next house, it startles the sleeping cat on the top stair. C2 are going to love delivering papers, and the neighbourhood cats will never be the same.

I'm a lot less determined and a much worse shot than my little brother.

On any other day, a day when a legendary and probably mythical fallen creature isn't leaving me burning feathers that will destroy me if I touch them, I'd enjoy watching C2. But not today. Everything is darker, the world is harder, scarier, the edge of town less inviting but more urgent than ever before.

If this is growing up, I'd like to avoid it. I really would.

Christine and Christopher deliver the papers, and I trail around behind them like any normal, paranoid, self-absorbed teenager. Do we all think we're being chased by deadly entities, I wonder?

Probably, but how many of us actually are?

Then Mom takes them out to the mall to buy some last minute back-to-school stuff, and I can't be alone another second, so I call Jez but she's not home. I can't stay alone, so I wander over to the library and spend the afternoon with a book that's been on my "to be read" list for a while: *The Adventures of Huckleberry Finn*.

I can't put it down, and when the library closes, I sign it out and take it with me. On the way home, I try not to look everywhere for burning feathers or strain to hear my name on the wind. I can't wait to get into my room and follow Huck downriver. I read all night, and I have to say, that boy Huck and his friend Jim have some strange adventures. Almost as strange as mine.

On Monday morning as I head to school, Mom stops me.

"I'm picking you up at school, out front, 3:35." I do a mental check. I don't have a doctor or dentist appointment for months. We've already bought everything I need for school.

"Why?" My mother looks uncomfortable. C2 race past us and out the front door to wait in the car. She watches them go.

"Mrs. Abernathy got us in to see Dr. Adam Parks really quickly. We start family therapy today." My stomach drops. I'm about to wail WHAT? WHY DO I HAVE TO GO? but my mother puts her hand up before I can say it.

"Don't argue, Gwen. It's *family* therapy. The doctor is expecting everyone to go the first time."

My whole body sinks.

I get through the day somehow. There's no gym class, so no Shelley Norman, and no science class, so no Martin Evells. I'm starting to get the hang of the rest of my classes, English, French, math, civics (which was mainly about salt and garbage in middle school and doesn't seem any better in grade nine), geography. I also don't see Everton anywhere, which is just as well because I can't imagine what I'd say to him.

In pottery class I stare at my "creation," which is another blob of unformed clay. Jez nicely helps me "create" an ashtray because clearly I can't do anything myself. I keep dropping the clay on the floor. When she asks me what's wrong all I can say is, "Family therapy today." Which is really only half the problem, but Jez doesn't know about the other half.

At the end of the day, I slouch across the high school lawn and hope no one sees me get into my mother's ancient car that roars and belches black smoke like the comedy car in a bad movie. I open the door, and my brother and sister shriek at me from the back seat. Together again, AND off school a little early on a Monday. What could be more exciting?

We drive downtown to the private health clinic that none of us has ever used, but then none of us has ever had therapy before. Not even after Dad died, I suddenly realize. No one thought of it.

My mother herds C2 into the waiting room and gets them signed up with the nice receptionist at the desk. The waiting room is filled with quiet little kids and their mothers, a few fathers too. There is no one even remotely close to my age here. I hang out by the door ready to bolt, my library copy of *Huckleberry Finn* clutched against me. I can hide behind a book, can't I?

My mother drags me over to a hard plastic waiting-room seat. I'm silent. I said everything I had to say in the car. Loudly.

Still, there is just no reason for me to be here. I open my book and read as stonily as I can. My brother and sister have commandeered the toy box and are loudly building an army of blocks across the floor. They're annoying everyone in the waiting room, and I think, *Good, everyone will see how normal they are and we can leave.* I have bigger problems, like, WAY bigger problems than my little brother and sister.

Dumb David Dumber whispers in my head.

Oh yeah.

Eventually a man comes into the waiting area and calls, "Mrs. Golden? Christopher and Christine?" Then he sees me and adds, "Gwendolyn?" as an after-thought. My brother and sister pop their heads up like jackrabbits, drop their blocks, and bolt through the door. The man smiles as they race into the room behind him then shakes my mother's hand and intro-duces himself as Dr. Adam Parks.

Dr. Adam Parks is annoyingly young. And worse still, distressingly nice. But I stay silent and stormy. I remind myself that he's the enemy; he's making me come to therapy for no reason.

I take a seat beside my mother and stow *Huck-leberry Finn* in my bag. Dr. Adam Parks sits across from us. Between us is a small table covered with snap-together toys, modelling clay in tubes, paper and pencil crayons, books, and a few strangely shaped blocks that I immediately want to pick up and investigate, but I don't. Along one side of the room is a table with a train set on it. C2 are already deep in conversation about who lives in the toy train village, blissfully building a new imaginary world. You'd think they might realize they should say hello to the person in charge of the room, but nope. Nothing. Just more twinned oblivion on their part.

My mom tries to corral them, but Dr. Adam Parks just laughs.

"I want to meet you two first anyway," he says. I clamp my mouth shut. My mom talks for a while, and Dr. Adam Parks writes down a few things, but mostly he appears to be listening. Nodding. Asking a few questions here and there. My mother tells him everything. About how C2 have always done well in school. Always been together. That we were worried that separating them might not be the best idea. She talks and talks then stops, embarrassed. It must be a relief for her to have someone to tell all this to. This has never occurred to me before.

On the other hand, I haven't said a word. I've been watching Dr. Adam Parks very closely. I could tell you how many hairs he has on his upper lip, I've observed him so well.

What can this person possibly know about me? And what am I going to tell him? How exactly do you tell a therapist that you can fly? Or that a Rogue fallen spirit is following you? That doesn't seem like something you could ever, ever share unless you wanted to be committed to a hospital somewhere. So this is an exercise in lying right from the start.

Suddenly the conversation has stopped, and I realize that Dr. Adam Parks is looking at me. He asks, "Well, Gwendolyn? What do you think?"

I blink. "What do I think? About what?"

"Gwendolyn, please pay attention!" my mother says, exasperated. She's obviously embarrassed with me, with my not listening.

Dr. Adam Parks says, "It's okay."

"No. Just tell me, what do I think about what?" I'm getting mad. My foot starts to jiggle. A few months ago, this might have meant the beginning of an uncontrollable flying jag. But not now. Now I have more control. Suddenly this makes me a little sad. It might be nice to shoot up to the ceiling in a rage right at the moment.

My mother is about to tell me to be polite, I can tell, but Dr. Adam Parks speaks fast.

"About your dad? Do you think your dad's death has affected your little brother and sister?" I stare at him. I think my mouth is open. Okay, who said he could say anything about my dad? Who told him he could go right there?

It's none of his business.

"I have no idea what you mean," I say as acidly as I can. Then I pick up my backpack and walk out of the room. I just leave the building. I walk down the front steps and out onto the main street.

No one comes after me, and I keep walking. Therapy session over. I just walk, and as I cross the streets and the parks and wander past the schools and buildings I've known all my life, I have an intense, burning thought.

Dr. Adams Parks just doesn't get to know about my dad. Not ever.

And what would I tell him anyway?

EIGHTEEN

I spend the next few hours walking around town, trying not to think. Not about therapy. Not about Martin Evells and Mr. McGillies. Definitely not about Everton or the Spirit Flyer. Or the Rogue.

When I get home, my mom doesn't mention my vanishing act. At dinner, my family talks about Dr. Adam Parks, but no one asks me what I did after I left the office. I pick at my salad and go to bed early.

The next day, high school starts for real.

In gym class, Shelley Norman won't leave me alone. We're playing field hockey, and my shins and ankles are black and blue. Every time Shelley tackles me with her wooden field hockey stick, I have another bruise. I'm going to be the limping kid all year.

Whenever I see Shelley in the hallways, Everton has his arm over her shoulders. He says hello with a grin, and she gives me a little stab-of-hatred look. They're like a two-headed dog, one that snarls and one that licks your hand.

Pottery class is interesting, even if I can't stand wearing Shelley's smock. There's something grossly encouraging about sliding your hands around in a lump of clay. It can become anything. When I finally fashion my first lopsided clay goblet, I'm oddly proud, prouder than I should be.

At the end of each class, we explain our creative efforts to Chas before we leave. If it's a sculpture, we talk about "presence and absence," which is the main reason I'll never try a sculpture, because I have no idea what that means. If it's a bowl or cup, he puts water in it to see if it leaks. I hold my first hideous creation, a mug, out to Chas. He pours a little water into it, and I hold my breath. Sure enough, a second later the water just drains away out the bottom. My creation leaks. He shrugs and says, "Next week, Gwendolyn."

I stick my leaky effort on the shelf above my name in the neatly labelled "Gwendolyn's Creation Space" and head off to my next class.

On Friday, I slide into my seat beside Martin Evells just as class starts.

"Hi," he whispers. He passes me a sheet about our first assignment.

"Plant cells," he says.

Plants.

Okay.

You know who has a lot of plants around his house, Martin? Mr. McGillies. Because he lives in a cornfield. Do you know him, Martin? I think you do. Quite well.

The bell rings, Mr. Tupperman tells us to take our seats, and we sit quietly to learn about plants. And it's too hard to concentrate. I simply can't.

There is so much unsaid between Martin and me. This isn't going to work. I squirm in my seat and stare down the eyepiece of a microscope at some weirdly shaped cells, which I try to draw. Clearly, I'm as bad at drawing plant cells as I am at shaping clay. When the hour is up, I've tried so hard not to touch Martin or make eye contact with him that I'm a nervous wreck.

When the bell rings, I bolt out of my chair, which falls over.

Martin, the gentleman, picks it up as the rest of the class files past us.

"Gwen, we need … we probably should talk." He smiles this crooked grin that I've always loved. I don't bark at him, so he goes on.

"Do you want to meet at The Float Boat tonight? At eight?" he asks. I can't think of how to say no, so I nod. "Yes, sure."

I walk C2 home after school. Jez is off at a dentist appointment, so I can't talk to her about the impending meeting with Martin. We stop at The Float Boat like we do every Friday. My little brother and sister roar around, stuffing jelly beans into candy bags while I watch. Mr. and Mrs. Forest see me and wave hello, but they're too busy with the Friday after-school crowd to chat. Just as well. I wave back. I have a feeling if I started talking to Mrs. Forest about what was going on in my Night Flying life, I'd never stop. And she'd be scared and worried and tell me not to fly out to Mr. McGillies's cabin.

If she doesn't know what's out there, she can't forbid me to go, can she?

After dinner, I'm a sweaty, horrible ball of lumpen clay. I have a date with Martin. Is that what it is? No matter how much I knead and tug at myself, I cannot seem to shape my thoughts or my body into anything resembling Gwendolyn Golden. At least, not the Gwendolyn Golden I'd like to be.

I phone Jez and tell her about Martin. Her face is still frozen from the dentist, so she's a bit slurry and hard to understand, but our conversation goes something like this:

Me: "I can't do this."

Jez: "Yesh, you can."

Me: "No, I really can't."

Jez: "Gwendolyn, lishen to me. You CAN talk to Martin. You HAVE to talk to Martin. You are his shience partner, you have to share a lab desk with him ALL YEAR. There's the small matter of the Worst Kiss Ever. And let's not forget his mother phoned the police on you and started rumours. You have to talk to him. And it's not necessarily a date."

Me: "I can't do this."

Jez: "Yesh, you can."

Me: "No, I can't."

We go on like this for a while. Then I say, "Maybe I can talk about the kiss. About his mom. It would be nice to hear an apology about both of those things. But … I can't do this."

"Yesh, you can." Eventually we grind to a halt, and she ends the conversation with a half-hearted "Good luck, call me when you get home." Then that's it.

I'm on my own.

It takes me a long time to get ready. Far too long. I wear the new jeans Mom got me for the start of school, running shoes, and my swishy green shirt she gave me for my birthday. My hair, well there's only so much I can do with heavy, wavy hair.

At seven thirty, I tell Mom I'm going out, and since she and C2 are deep into a game of Monopoly, she waves goodbye and tells me to be home by eleven or call.

What exactly will I call with, Mom? I don't have a phone, remember?

As the door shuts behind me, I realize I'm missing board game night. When did I get so forgetful about board game night? I love board game night. First my paper route and now board games left behind on the growing heap of my childhood. What's next?

I step out of the house and resist the urge to look up and scan the sky. Instead, I hold my father's gold feather around my neck. It's a beautiful fall night, and cool air gently blows against my skin. Stars start to come out. I can hear kids playing road hockey a few streets over. I round the corner to The Float Boat and stop dead.

Everton Miles walks toward me.

"Jeesh, Gwen, don't look so happy to see me," he teases. He stops in front of me, and I try not to notice how nice he looks.

"Hello, Everton. Can I help you?"

"You look nice," he says. How like him to be disarming.

"Thanks. I have to go."

"Your date is waiting for you in The Float Boat," he says quietly. How does he know about Martin?

"It's not a date. He's my science partner."

"Okay, well, whatever you want to call him, Mr. McGillies's helper is wearing seriously too much body spray. You may want to keep your distance." He says this with glee.

"Tell me what you want, Everton."

He gets serious. "Look, just don't go out to the cabin with him, okay? There's the … you know." He drops his voice even lower. "It's dangerous, Gwen. I'm not kidding. Stay away from there."

I narrow my eyes.

"I can call Celestine, remember? You were out there alone with just her. And if it's so dangerous, why didn't you tell Mrs. Forest about it, or anyone else?" I try not to ask myself the same question. Everton hesitates before he answers me.

"I don't want to bring the entire Night Flyer community down on us for a Rogue trial unless it's real. I'm still trying to gather evidence. You say you've seen it, but Celestine and I haven't, not really. But you shouldn't go near there, not alone." He actually sounds a bit worried about me.

"Well, if I'm with Martin, I won't be alone, will I?" The clock in the town hall down the street starts to chime. It's eight o'clock. His dark blue eyes hold mine. It's unnerving.

The last bell chimes.

I head onto the front porch of The Float Boat. His final words drift out of the darkness. "Just don't go out there, Gwendolyn Golden. For me."

Why would I do anything for you, Everton Miles?

I square my shoulders and walk into the store.

NINETEEN

BODY SPRAY!

Everton is right. I can smell Martin from across the store. I take a final big breath of clean air and slide into the booth with him. Mrs. Forest brings us both a float and says hello with a wink. I hate floats. She knows that, but Martin doesn't and must have bought this for me. I take a polite sip and gag.

I still hate floats.

Mrs. Forest vanishes into the back, and we're alone. Martin takes a big sip and then clears his throat. "You look nice," he says.

"Thanks." I consider giving him a tip about using less body spray, but it's too late to help in the current situation, and it would just embarrass him. He takes another sip.

"Gwen, I've wanted to talk to you all summer, but I was too scared, I guess. Now we're science partners, we have to. I'm really sorry."

"Sorry?"

"You know what I mean." He's sheepish. He takes another long drink of float and won't look up.

"What are you sorry for?" I prompt. He takes a deep breath and finds something on the wall beside us fascinating.

"First of all, I'm really sorry my mom started a rumour about you. I know you don't do drugs. You wouldn't believe the arguments we had all summer about it. I even made her tell her church group the truth. I watched her say that you weren't a drug addict, that she was wrong. I'm really sorry she phoned the police on you, too. I begged her not to."

He takes another embarrassed sip of his float. He certainly seems sorry. It must have taken a lot of determination to get Mrs. Evells to confess to her church group, but maybe they confess stuff like that all the time. I wouldn't know.

"Okay, thank you. It was interesting when the police showed up."

There's a silence and more staring at the wall, so I finally ask, "Are you sorry for anything else?"

Martin looks more uncomfortable, if that's possible, and he's saved for a moment by a young family that walks into the store. The kids run over to the huge barrel of lollipops and pick out their favourite flavours. They're loud.

Martin lowers his voice.

"Yes. I'm really sorry that I stopped being your friend when we were little, Gwen." We finally make eye contact, and he looks anguished.

"I wish I could say that was my mom's fault, too. It was, partly. But to be honest, I thought it was weird that your dad disappeared. I was really worried that my dad would disappear, too. I was a little kid, it scared me. The truth is, I look back at those times when we played all summer in my backyard, and I think I was happy because of you. Happier than I would have been without you."

I'm shocked at this piece of self-revelation. My hand creeps toward my father's golden feather, but I catch myself and stop. Martin looks at me with such hope that he'll be forgiven.

"There's one more thing. You need to apologize for one more thing."

He's puzzled. He's coming up blank.

"In your playhouse? Last summer? The Worst Kiss Ever?" I prompt. His whole body sinks.

"Oh, that." He turns away. His cheeks turn a deep pink blush. "I'm too ashamed to think about it. I'm really, really sorry about that. I am." He looks at his hands in his lap.

The little kids behind me make a lot of noise. The youngest girl shouts, "LemonLemonLemon!" at the top of her voice. It reminds me that once upon a time Martin used to smell like lemons. A nice, sweet, clean smell I always loved. Adolescence has made him abandon his own natural scent. I've almost gotten used to the body spray, but I've been breathing through my mouth.

Martin looks miserable. I could just leave now and somehow manage science class all year. But the truth is, I like this boy. I do. Despite everything.

"It's not your fault that your mother called the police on me or started a rumour. And I guess if your father disappeared when we were little, I might have been scared too. But as for the playhouse last summer … if you want to kiss someone, just ask first."

He nods. "Yeah, of course. Don't worry. I promise. That'll never happen again, ever."

I feel like an enormous weight has just been removed from my very soul. But I'm not done, and I lower my voice.

"And thanks for not telling anyone. About me. About, you know." I look slowly up at the ceiling, as though I'm watching something float up there.

He pulls himself as close as he can to me across the table and drops his voice to a whisper. "Why, *whatever* do you mean, Gwendolyn Golden?" He's got a wicked little grin and a glint in his eye that I remember all too well. My six-year-old self giggles, which is hardly very grown up, but I can't help it.

Then we sit and talk through another float for Martin and two plates of French fries, then a cup of tea each. We talk about school, we talk about his favourite sport (soccer) and my favourite sport (I don't really have one except flying), we talk about books (he's read way more than me). At nine thirty, he looks at his watch.

"Oh, I have to go. I have to see a friend."

"Who?" I'm suddenly wary.

"Do you know the old bottle man? Mr. McGillies? A few friends and I have been helping him. Tonight is my night to go to his cabin. Do you want to come?"

TWENTY

I have no self-control. I have no right to be doing what I'm doing. I've been warned against it by a fellow Night Flyer, a Spirit Flyer, and by every bit of good sense I have at my disposal. Even *Your First Flight: A Night Flyer's Handbook (The Complete & Unabridged Version, Newly Updated!)* warned me to be careful.

I shouldn't be here. But here I am.

Martin and I walk along the dark road to Mr. McGillies's cabin.

It's a gorgeous night. The stars blaze in the clear black sky. The corn waves gently in the breeze and sets up a constant rustle and chatter. Harvest is coming. I've called Celestine in my head a few times and even whispered her name out loud when Martin was too far away to hear. So far she hasn't announced her arrival, but maybe she wouldn't. I've never called her before, so I have no idea. I might see a golden shimmer at the corner of my eye now and then, but I could be imagining it.

I can tell Martin wants to hold my hand, but I keep mine firmly in my pocket. I don't need any sweaty hand-holding right now, not so soon after the sweetness of all those apologies. Besides, now we've cleared the air between us, I feel like a little kid again and close to Martin in a way that has nothing to do with holding hands.

This is the night of amazing things: sincere apologies that make up for a lot of sadness. Plus, I'm about to find out about why Martin is with Mr. McGillies. There's the Rogue, of course. And the small problem of Mr. McGillies being my Watcher, but it's not something I absolutely have to share. I'm still not completely ready to discuss the whole Night Flyer thing with Martin.

We see the light shining in Mr. McGillies's cabin down the lane, and Martin stops. His eyes brighten. "Can you show me?" He puts his arms out at his sides, like a bird.

I look around, put my faith in Celestine, then take a little run down the lane and lift into the air, light as a feather. For once I manage a graceful take-off. Martin laughs and watches. I buzz over his head, and he jumps to swat my foot. We both laugh, and I buzz him a few more times while he takes more playful swipes at my feet. I get a little giddy and decide to show off. I zoom really high, really fast, but not so high that he can't see me. He's below me, a little dot on the road just past my left toe, waving. I hear him laugh. Far below me, the light in Mr. McGillies's cabin shines, and I smell wood smoke from the chimney.

Then the Rogue walks out of the corn.

He stands behind Martin in the laneway, so Martin doesn't see him.

Martin raises his hand in a wave, and the feathered man copies him and raises his hand, too. His eyes are golden, his wings outspread, his darkness complete.

I try to scream, to tell Martin to run, but no words come out. Then the Rogue puts his head back in a silent, mocking laugh, and I hear the corn whisper my name.

Gwendolyn....

TWENTY-ONE

I land with a thud and grab Martin's hand.

"RUN!"

And we do. I look over my shoulder once, but there's no feathered man. There's nothing but laneway and tall corn ... but then for a second a shimmer of white light hovers over the road then disappears.

Or maybe not. I'm too scared to look again.

We tear toward the cabin then slump against the wall, breathless.

"You still can't outrun me!" Martin thought this was a game? He thought I was kidding? I try to catch my breath, and my heart pounds. The cabin door opens, and a familiar head pops out.

It's Everton.

He smiles and says, "Hi Martin, hi Gwen! I wondered when you'd get here! Mr. McGillies is having his dinner."

My mouth falls open, and for a second I am completely unglued. Did time shift? Did I get lost in some weird fantasy? From behind Martin's back,

I point down the road and mouth, "The FEATH-ERED MAN! THE ROGUE!" but Everton turns his back on me before he can notice.

Then I want to scream, *Everton, what are you doing here?*

My next thought stops me cold. If Shelley Norman is in there with Mr. McGillies, I'm leaving right now, Rogue or no Rogue! But Everton ignores me and talks to Martin like he's known him forever.

"He really likes the soup you made, Martin," Everton says. We all step into the cabin, and Mr. McGillies is sitting on the couch, alone. He smiles and waves at me. No Shelley Norman.

"Hi, missy!" He eats soup off a tray on his knees. He's a shadow of himself, small and thin, and I'm hit by guilt. Why haven't I come to see him? I'm terrible to my Watcher. I say hello, but I keep my distance.

Mr. McGillies eats Martin's soup while Martin flits around the kitchen getting us tea. When he's out of earshot, I round on Everton.

"I just saw the Rogue!" I hiss quietly. "And what are you doing here?" Everton is astonished and blinks at me with huge eyes.

"You *did*? Are you *sure*? Is Celestine out there?"

"I'm not sure. Maybe. I didn't stick around to check!" We're clearly whispering about something urgent, and we jump apart because Martin enters the room with a tinkling tea tray.

"You two know each other?" he says, handing out tea. Everton shrugs.

"We have some old friends in common. I was just telling her I'm helping you with the gardening project. Didn't you see the posters at school, Gwendolyn? Didn't Miss Moreau talk to you?"

"No, I didn't see the posters. No, Miss Moreau didn't talk to me."

Martin puts down his teacup. I can see he's wondering how I could possibly have old friends in common with the new boy in town, but he's polite. Instead he says, "We're almost finished the garden. Do you want to see?"

Garden? Gardening project? What are they talking about? I exchange a look with Everton, but what are we going to say? We can hardly not go out to see whatever it is that has them both here.

We leave Mr. McGillies with his soup, and Everton and I follow Martin to the back of Mr. McGillies's cabin. We're both nervous as Martin talks away.

"We worked really hard on it. It's taken since the start of school."

We round the cabin and stop dead. I can see strange shapes looming in the yard and hear a gentle chiming. Martin plugs in a big outdoor cable, and a thousand tiny white lights spring to life. I gasp: a glass garden leaps out of the darkness. Trees, bushes, tables, chairs, and benches glisten and shine in the dark, lit up and sparkling. Everything is entirely made of glass.

Martin and Everton have created a garden paradise of glass bottles. It looks like fairyland.

A perfect archway of bottles frames the field. A wheelbarrow, rakes, and shovels lean up against the cabin.

"How did you do all this?" I ask. Martin looks ridiculously proud.

"Everton was a big help. Miss Moreau supervised and got volunteers and tools together, and we get community hours for the work. A lot of kids helped out this week."

"Shelley Norman helped all last weekend," Everton says evenly, looking at me. I close my eyes for a second.

"And Jeffrey Parks was here, too, and a big kid named Sebastian and a few others. Mr. Forest came and helped us make a table and benches out of the bottles." I walk over to the nearest glass bench and look at it, unsure. Martin nods. "Sit down, it's comfortable."

I sit. The bottles point into the soil, half dug into the ground. Then the next few layers of bottles are on top of that, tightly wired together. There's a smooth board across the last row of bottles for a bench. The table is entirely made of bottles with gaps where the bottles don't touch. Everton says, "We aren't quite finished. The table top is still to come."

I walk over to one of the sparkling glass bushes lit with tea lights. The bottles rattle and chime gently with the wind. It's magical.

The mountain of bottles I saw with Everton that first night is gone. "You used all Mr. McGillies's bottles? He had thousands."

"Over five thousand, actually. We used about half of them in the garden, and the rest we put in Everton's brother's truck and drove to the recycling centre while Mr. McGillies wasn't looking," Martin says. "But he wasn't too upset. He got about one hundred and fifty dollars for the glass and donated it to the men's homeless shelter. He has some friends there." I walk over to the glass archway, which is cleverly pieced together in an interlocking pattern. I look out into the dark fields.

"Why? Why did you do all this for Mr. McGillies?"

Martin clears his throat, but Everton speaks first. "He's sick, Gwen."

Martin nods. "Really sick."

Part of me knew what they were going to say. My Watcher hasn't been watching me lately. I've been watching him. I scan the lovely bottle garden, listen to the sweet bell sound of the swaying bottles, watch the sparkling glass.

Of course Mr. McGillies is sick. I knew that somehow. Which is why I've avoided him. Which is why he hasn't been rattling around town except on the first day of school. I realize with a lurch that maybe he was looking for me that day to tell me.

My Watcher is deathly ill.

Then ...

Gwendolyn ...

The Rogue appears outside the bottle archway. For a second all three of us are completely still, and the only movement is the gentle shushing of the stalks behind dark feathers. Then the Rogue strides toward me and sweeps me up into the dark sky.

The last thing I hear is Everton scream. Or maybe it's Martin.

It's also entirely possible that the scream comes from me.

TWENTY-TWO

I'm lying on a beach beside a lake.

Leafy trees sway in a gentle breeze. I sit up and try to focus. A figure walks toward me across the beach sand and small pebbles. For a moment I see a dark, feathered creature, then a man stops in front of me. I'm afraid to look up.

Gwendolyn Golden, I'm pleased to finally meet you.

He has a very deep voice. He squats down in front of me, and there's really nothing I can do except look at him. I'm not in my body. I'm somewhere over the lake, watching myself talk to a creature on a beach.

The Rogue.

There are no deep, golden eyes now. His eyes are just clear and green. No black feathers either, just a black T-shirt and jeans on a human body. A nice face looks back at me. He looks a bit like Mr. Tupperman, to be honest. The only thing a little odd about him is a too-sweet smell and his bare feet, which are perfectly white, like marble. The whole place is too sweet-smelling, though, like it's masking something.

Allow me to introduce myself. I'm Abilith.

He raises his eyebrows and offers his hand to help me stand. I don't take it, but I do stand up and brush the sand off my jeans.

"You're a Rogue Spirit Flyer. From the *Night Flyer's Handbook*. From the legend of Abilith and Mirandel."

Part of me is saying, *Gwendolyn, run!* But a bigger part of me is asleep somehow, as though I'm merely a spectator. My body is just sleepwalking through whatever is going on here. It's the strangest sensation.

Yes. I'm Abilith of the legend. I'm surprised you've heard of me. You must be doing your reading.

He chuckles, and it's a deep, soothing sound.

You have nothing to fear, Gwendolyn. You are safe.

There's not much I can do if I'm not, a snappy part of me thinks. The real Gwendolyn is still in there somewhere — that's good to know.

"Where are we?" I ask. I look out over the beautiful lake, the lovely blue summer sky, toward the green and gently waving trees. It's pretty, but there's something a little off about it. The air is too sweet, the trees are too green, the sky too perfectly blue and mirrored too exactly in the calm water.

This is my place. My shore. My home. You're safe here, although we may not have much time.

He brushes his hand through his black hair. It's a simple enough movement, but it's mesmerizing. It's like watching a gorgeous animal perfectly at ease with itself, rippling with life and terror. A tiger maybe. A leopard. A shark.

Shall we walk?

We walk along the sand. My feet are bare, too, for some reason, and the sand is warm between my toes. It's the only sensation I can feel, since everything from my feet up is still fast asleep or unconscious.

Would you like to know why I brought you here?

"Yes."

Forget whatever you have heard. No doubt you've read that I'm a terrible creature, fallen, a thing to shun and fear. I'm not. And that whole myth about me not liking groups of people is not true. I just choose not to disrupt. I'm thoughtful that way most of the time. I'm different, yes, I'm not like my brothers and sisters the Spirit Flyers, yes, but I've never hurt anyone.

"What about Mirandel? You stole her, and she vanished forever." I'm starting to feel oddly misplaced, like part of me is missing. I notice my teeth are chattering softly, but I'm not cold. I'm not anything.

Abilith stoops to pick up a stick on the beach, and with one simple, elegant swing of his arm, he sends it soaring over the water. It lands with a shimmery scattering of water-filled sunlight and a gentle, distant splash.

Mirandel. The lovely girl. Oh, that she could have lived forever. She was part mortal, Gwendolyn, and lived a mortal's short existence. She's been gone a long time, too long, forever, it seems. But I didn't steal her or keep her here against her will.

"Is that why I'm here? Because you miss Mirandel?"

He looks at me, surprised.

You do look remarkably like her. And you're a strong spirit like she was, that I can see. But I'd never keep you here against your will, Gwendolyn Golden. You do HAVE free will, you know, regardless of what others may tell you. All this nonsense about handbooks and making a choice about your future, you don't have to do any of it. All you really have to do is fly, if that is your wish.

I look into his odd green eyes. They aren't human eyes, of course, but they're a very clever copy. We stare at each other. There's something wrong with Abilith's pupils. They keep rapidly changing size, big, little, big, little. It's like watching his heartbeat, if he has one.

"Can you please hurry up and get to why I'm here?"

Yes, of course, my apologies. If you know who I am, then you know that I'm a Spirit Flyer, or once was. I have their skill, their vision, I'm like them in every way except one: they have cast me out. Don't ask why. I may tell you one day, just not today.

I was. I was about to ask him why. A school of fish swims below the surface of the lake, churning the water with their tails, silver bellies flashing toward the sun. A fish leaps out of the water and snaps a dragonfly from the air. I gasp. For a second, the fish sheds sun-spangled water with the dragonfly struggling and flickering in its jaw. Then the pair sink with a loud splash below the water.

Abilith doesn't seem to notice.

"You still haven't told me why I'm here. You're keeping me against my will."

You are free to go at any time, Gwendolyn. And no doubt my clumsy sister Celestine will arrive at any moment to claim you anyway. She is very easy to deceive, I'm afraid, and not very bright. But know this: I've brought you here to tell you the truth about someone you have lost. There are others who want to keep the truth from you, but I see no reason to hide it. They say they are protecting you, but I say you need to know. Do you want to know?

I look into the odd green eyes.

I know the truth about your father, Gwendolyn. About the night he died. Do you want to know the truth, too?

A flash of anger spears me, and I wake up. He wants to tell me about my father? He doesn't get to mention my father.

"Whatever you have to tell me is probably lies. And you're the last, well, not person, but creature I guess, who I want to talk to about anything, especially not my father. Take me back. Now."

There's a dull thumping in my ears. Is that my heartbeat now? I'm glad it's still there, pumping away. Good to be reminded that I still have a body.

Despite my protest, Abilith speaks again.

You should know, Gwendolyn. You deserve to know. It is your story. No one can withhold your story. Here is the truth. Your father died saving someone you know. He went out into the storm to check on a neighbour, so the story goes. Do you ever wonder which neighbour? Are you not curious?

Miserable me, miserable fatherless daughter, miserable one who has always, always wondered that very thing. Oh, miserable head that nods ever so slightly and miserable lips that part to whisper, "Yes!"

In the next instant, a cloud shimmers above the lake and bursts into an image of a dark night and a terrible storm.

My father stands in the middle of a laneway beside a cornfield. He covers his eyes as rain slicks his hair to his head. He leans into the fierce wind, calling a name into the storm. I can hear his voice, but not the words. His raincoat whips wildly behind him in the darkness, and he reaches a hand toward a cabin in the distance with a light on.

My father stands in the exact spot beside the cornfield that I have visited all summer.

It's the spot where I watch the light in Mr. McGillies's window every night. My father calls into the storm again and again, and this time I hear him: *McGovern McGillies! McGovern McGillies!*

Then my father finds the frightened old man cowering beside the road, and he helps Mr. McGillies get up. The two men struggle toward the cabin in the howling rain. Then …

… oh, miserable me who has to see what happens next. But I cannot look away.

A dark cloud descends on them both, blotting out the cornfield. They disappear. I want to scream, but I can't. Nothing comes out.

Mr. McGillies falls to the muddy road, out of the cloud, and claws his way into the cabin. My father's feet vanish as he's swept up into the black, black heart of the storm. I've seen this cloud before. T. Bosch saw it, too.

Abilith says it for me with a whisper. *The Shade found them, Gwendolyn.*

He says this so gently, so sweetly. His green eyes look almost compassionate, weirdly pulsing and almost believably filled with sadness.

Your father fought bravely. He struggled against the Shade, but he could not fly hard and fast enough to save them both. Your father saved Mr. McGillies, then the Shade swept him away.

I've wondered all my life exactly how my father died, and now I know. Who was the neighbour? Where did my father's body go? How did it happen?

I bow my head. A huge tear wells up and spills onto my cheek.

Drip.

I'm in my body now, fully frightened, fully awake, completely aware.

Why is knowledge so painful? My father sacrificed himself to save Mr. McGillies? I open my mouth but nothing comes out, and I'm pretty sure that this is the very moment that my heart breaks. I feel it, a bursting and pulsing outward, the death of everything that I didn't want to know.

The birth of everything I now know forever.

I can't ever go back to not knowing the truth.

More huge tears slowly roll down my cheeks.

Abilith stands beside me, opening and closing his hands, as though he has no idea how to comfort me. Clearly he's good at getting the truth out there but useless at mopping up the mess afterward. He doesn't even try to comfort me but watches the sky over the water.

He's edgy, uneasy, and paces the beach in front of me.

The sky changes from blue to a violent roiling black, with clouds billowing and spilling and swooping down toward us. It looks like a T. Bosch drawing, a dark, dangerous, terrifying sky come to life. Abilith tenses beside me and then shouts. He throws his arms above his head as though shielding us.

NO!

A brilliant light blinds me. I cover my face. Whatever force was keeping me calm and distant has vanished, and I'm fully aware of my terror. My hand reaches to my heart, and there's my father's golden feather. I clasp it with everything I have.

A blast of wind tears the beach apart, and sand whips my skin and fills my nostrils so I can't breathe. I cower beneath Abilith, who is no longer the harmless-looking man in a black T-shirt and jeans.

He's a ferocious, howling wind with a black body and feathers of fire on his shoulders. His golden eyes blaze, and he fills the air with shrieking that freezes my soul.

White feathers charge out of the storm toward us. A blazing whiteness lands on the beach and runs headlong into Abilith. For a second, two whirling shapes, one white and one black, twist and form together. Swords clash in the darkness, again and again. More bright white figures arrive from the sky, and the air above me is filled with bodies colliding, fighting, slashing, forming, and unforming in black-and-white smoke.

The lake, the sky, the trees, everything is gone, and it's just me alone in the wilderness. Above are the battling creatures of light and dark, and I couldn't tell you how long I huddle on the sand, listening to the shrieks and bellows and crash of swords above my head. I think time is irrelevant at this point, to be honest. Abilith shrieks once again, then everything is blackness and silence.

Then … a Spirit Flyer forms above me.

Gwendolyn Golden! Gwendolyn Golden!

Something moves against my skin, but I can't tell if my eyes are open or closed. The world has contracted and there is no colour, no sound, nothing at all.

Then everything hurts, and the ground is beneath me. I open my eyes.

You are safe, Gwendolyn Golden.

The brilliant white Spirit Flyer lays me down gently at the edge of the dark cornfield.

"Celestine. You saved me," I whisper.

Sleep now, little golden sister. I must help my brothers and sisters catch the Rogue.

A flurry of white feathers vanishes in a stream of gold light above my head, and she's gone.

I turn my head to see Mr. McGillies's bottle archway glitter and gleam with tea lights, his cabin in the distance. Two boys run toward me, and I hear them call my name.

And then I faint, or maybe it's dying?

TWENTY-THREE

Not dying. Not dead. In fact, quite alive.

I open my eyes. Everton runs up, then Martin. For a moment no one moves, and we're a weird tableau, three humans blinking at each other in the tea lights with the gentle ping-ping of bottles swaying in the garden.

"Gwen! Are you okay?" Everton whispers. He looks so stricken that I pull myself together and stand up.

"Yes, I think so." I'm not, but I'm a good liar.

"What *was* that thing?" Martin asks.

"It's a long story, Martin," Everton says. "We'll tell you, but go say goodnight to Mr. McGillies now. We have to take Gwen home." Martin frowns and then reluctantly leaves us by the cabin door. Everton whirls on me.

"Gwen, what happened?"

I'm weary, and I feel sick. I lean against the cabin. I've never felt so tired in my life.

"It was the Rogue. Abilith. The one from the legend."

"It was? *Abilith*? Really?"

I nod, distant. "He took me to his world and showed me ... I was there a long time."

Everton shakes his head. "No Gwen, you were gone a few seconds. The Rogue snatched you, I chased him into the cornfield, and then Celestine brought you back to the archway a few moments later. What did he show you?"

"Nothing. I'll tell you later. What do we tell Martin?"

Martin appears at the cabin door and shuts it quietly. "Why don't you tell me the truth?" he says. He sounds concerned but deadly serious. Everton and I exchange looks, but we can see we have to tell him. He clearly saw two Spirit Flyers, one light and one dark. What kind of a lie do you make up for something like that?

The three of us head home along the dark road, and Everton tells Martin everything. I have to say for a non-Night Flyer, Martin takes the truth about Celestine and Abilith remarkably well. He's not even that surprised to learn that Everton is a Night Flyer, too. He asks a lot of questions but seems to believe us. I don't tell them what Abilith showed me, though, and Everton doesn't ask again.

I'm silent, weak, struggling to stay on my feet and keep up with them. I do, but only because Everton has a strong, steadying arm around me, holding me up the whole way home.

TWENTY-FOUR

So begins my new life with too much knowledge.

I get up every morning and do what's expected of me. I go to school. I walk C2 home at the end of the day. I make them food, I do my homework, I walk my dog.

But everything is changed. I keep seeing my father's feet as they vanish into a dark cloud beside an old cabin.

Other than Everton and Martin, no one knows about Abilith. Everton has asked a few times but has politely received the message that I don't want to talk about it. Martin doesn't mention it again. I don't tell Jez, because she's so far out of the loop now. Where would I start? I also don't want Everton to tell Mrs. Forest what happened, and he's good to his word and keeps it quiet. No one knows the Rogue showed me the truth about my dad. I'm all alone with that knowledge, and who would I tell, anyway?

I carry the weight of it with me all the time.

It's a beautiful Saturday in October, one of those strange warm days that are still and clear. Cassie and I walk around town a little until I find myself in front of The Float Boat. The store is full of younger kids, and the noise and buzz of the place just doesn't appeal to me. I watch Mr. and Mrs. Forest serve floats and fries to a whole new batch of little kids from this town. I used to be one of them.

I head down the street, go around the corner, and bang into a lady. She drops her bag of groceries, and I stoop to help her pick them up.

It's Miss Moreau.

"Hi, Gwendolyn!" she says nicely, and I help her stuff her oranges back into the bag. She asks me how school is going, and we chat until suddenly we're at her front door.

I tell her I liked the work she, Martin, and Everton did on Mr. McGillies's bottle garden.

"The lights are nice, aren't they? They were Martin's idea. How is Mr. McGillies? Have you seen him?"

"No. Well, yes, but not much. Just once lately."

Miss Moreau stands on the step of her house and smiles. "He's a great guy. Mr. McGillies used to be my art teacher at the band council community centre when I was a kid. He was a sculptor. He won awards and travelled around the world doing art with underprivileged communities. But you probably know that. He showed me how to make glass bottle sculptures when I was young, so I'm glad I remembered how to do it in his own garden."

How did I not know that Mr. McGillies taught art to kids? Or that he was a world-travelling artist?

I help Miss Moreau get her groceries into the house, but I turn down her offer of iced tea, using Cassie as my excuse.

"I hope you come out for volleyball tryouts next week, Gwen, I think you'd be good on the team. Oh, and the bottle garden isn't finished. You can help us any time for community service hours."

"Thanks, but I'm a bit busy right now." I have zero interest in volleyball, plus I'm terrible at it, which she'll find out soon enough. And as for working in the bottle garden? I'm done with being swept into the air by legendary creatures. I'll find something else to do for community hours, thanks.

I say goodbye and walk away from Miss Moreau. There really are two of me.

One who knows the truth about my father.

And one who has to live in the world with everyone else.

TWENTY-FIVE

Weeks float by like leaves on a stream.

Daily routine is good, and going to classes and walking through the halls keeps my feet on the ground. Whenever I see Everton, he stops to chat, but only if Shelley isn't with him. If she is, they walk past. I keep starting conversations with Jez and then stopping.

I haven't flown since the night at Mr. McGillies's cabin, and Everton hasn't dropped by to tempt me. I guess we're both too scared.

In the past few weeks, Martin and I have gotten closer. He chats with me whenever we're alone in the halls, and we get along fine in science class. He walks home sometimes with Jez, C2, and me after school. Christopher likes Martin and tells him jokes. The two of them laugh all the way home, and I can't help thinking what a nice boy Martin is to hang out with my little brother and pretend he's funny. It's sweet to watch.

I fail my first science test. Mr. Tupperman returns our papers, and mine has no mark on it, just a note in red pen: *Gwendolyn, please see me after class.* Martin sees the note on my paper but politely looks away.

After class I go up to Mr. Tupperman.

"Gwendolyn, did you study for this test?" He raises an eyebrow and waits.

"I'll do better next time, sir, I promise."

"Okay, if you need extra help, you should let me know," he says kindly.

"I'll help Gwendolyn study, Mr. Tupperman," Martin says. I forgot he was there.

"You're still interested in tutoring, Martin?"

Martin nods.

"What do you think, Gwendolyn?"

I don't say no, so it's settled. Martin scribbles his number on a piece of paper and hands it to me. "Call me," he says and rushes away, and I get the feeling he's been dying to tutor me all along.

Too bad he can't help me in gym.

In gym, we've done a few weeks of field hockey, then badminton, then basketball, and now we've moved on to volleyball. I'm permanently black and blue, since Shelley is constantly kicking or slashing at me. I spend most of my time in gym class trying to avoid her. I can't help but notice that after that day with the oranges on the sidewalk, Miss Moreau hasn't breathed another word to me about joining the volleyball team. I can hardly blame her.

I'm terrible at volleyball.

I'm so bad that after a few gym classes, everyone stops making eye contact with me, even Jez. By the third volleyball class, I hear everyone take in a little breath whenever the ball comes to me. Everyone watches me miss the ball, again, and again, and again. And again. Eventually they just give up hope. I haven't touched the volleyball once, which is weird because I'm one of the tallest kids in the class, but whenever I go one way, the ball goes the other. There's some force in me that repels the ball.

It snows this morning on the way to school, not unusual for mid-November. I refuse to wear my winter boots, and I slip and slide on the icy sidewalks all the way. At the gates to school, I go down hard and bang my knee on the frozen ground. There's a tiny rip across the knee of my favourite jeans and the beginnings of a small bruise underneath. In gym class I do a little limp, hoping it'll land me on the bench with an ice pack for an hour.

But Miss Moreau won't let me sit out. I have to play volleyball. I rotate off the bench and into the first position and stare right into the piggy black eyes of Shelley Norman facing me across the net. The other girls are all nervous. They can maybe sense what's going to happen.

The ball gets served. I jump up, arms out ...

... and I don't miss. This is the day that my body decides to finally get volleyball. I actually touch the ball. But I don't just touch it — I smash it. And I don't just smash it to the floor for a point, but I accidentally smash it full force into Shelley Norman's face. Believe me, no one is more shocked than me. There's blood everywhere, spurting out of Shelley's nose and mouth, and she stares at me for a second.

For one quiet moment everyone holds their breath … then Shelley flings herself under the net.

She's going to kill me.

Shelley Norman lands on me, and I go down hard on my sore knee. I gasp and throw my arms up in defense, but my reflex move catches Shelley on the chin, and she looks shocked for a second then swats me. I catch it on the shoulder as I roll away.

Shelley's hot breath hits my face with a little daub of spit. She wants me dead. This is nothing like wearing her clay-covered smock in art class. This is war. I struggle to push her off, but she's bigger than I am by a lot. She slaps me across the face. Slap, slap.

There's a lot of screaming, legs and arms flailing. I hear a familiar voice shriek a terrible curse, and the room falls quiet.

It's me cursing.

It probably all takes ten seconds before Miss Moreau wades in and tears Shelley off me. Jez takes my hand and says urgently, "Come on, Gwen, stop!" There's blood all over Shelley's face, and I'm covered in it too, although I'm not sure if it's her blood or mine.

We both stagger to our feet and gasp for air like prizefighters. Then the gym doors open with a bang, and Mr. Skinty walks in, accompanied by two scared-looking girls from our class. Apart from heavy breathing from Shelley and me, the place is dead quiet.

"Miss Golden, Miss Norman, come with me please."

Without a word, Jez takes me by the arm, and Miss Moreau takes Shelley, and we march through the halls to the principal's office. Class is in, so no one is in the halls, except of course the one person who will get the most out of seeing us bloodied and beaten. Everton is out of class with a hall pass and watches us both walk by. I don't make eye contact. My face is stormy, not to mention bloody.

Shelley does, though, and snarls at him, "Your girlfriend is a wimp, Miles." He doesn't say anything, at least not that I can hear.

This strikes me as interesting, though. Why would Shelley think I'm his girlfriend?

We get to the principal's office and sink into the deep leather chairs that my brother and sister sat in a few months ago. Miss Moreau sits on one side with Shelley and Jez with me on the other.

Miss Moreau looks very concerned. Jez, too. Shelley doesn't say anything or look at me. She's got a tissue wadded against her cheek, a twin to the one I have wadded against my ear, which has a gash from one of Shelley's rings.

Mr. Skinty says, "Two-week suspension," and Jez says she thinks my mom is at work. I go to the washroom with Jez, who helps me clean up. She fusses and clucks, and we don't speak. Then I wait with Miss Moreau at the front door until my mother arrives in her old car a little while later. We drive away, and I see Shelley Norman walking home alone.

She still has the tissue wadded against her cheek, and it's covered in blood. I stopped bleeding some time ago.

TWENTY-SIX

Suspended. I'm suspended. It's a little like floating.

The first day I lie on my bed, staring at the ceiling. My mother is surprisingly calm about the whole thing, disappointed but not terribly angry. She says something like, "You do have a bad temper, Gwendolyn. I'm not delighted about this, of course, just don't let it happen again." And that's pretty much the extent of my punishment from her.

The first day, Jez comes by to talk after school, but I'm really not in the mood. She babbles on for a while. She says everyone is worried about me, but I seriously doubt that's true. I listen to her drone on about some guy in her math class who asked her out.

"You should go," I say.

She wrinkles her nose. "He's short."

"So? Is he nice?"

Jez considers this. "Yeah, I guess."

"Just go on a date with him, Jez. Who cares if he's short? Just look perfect and go on a STUPID DATE!"

This is harsh even for me, and Jez says, "Jeesh, Gwen, calm down. I'll ... I'll see you tomorrow, I guess." Then she takes her coat and leaves.

She comes the next day, and the next. She tells me about Chas, and she even brings me a little sculpture of a bird she made. It's pretty and I stick it in my window. I could talk to Jez. I *should* talk to Jez. But I don't.

I'm allowed out to get C2 after school every day, except the days that they have therapy then Mom picks them up. I lie around and watch TV, but there's nothing remotely interesting on in the daytime. I haven't read much since I finished *The Adventures of Huckleberry Finn,* since nothing else will ever be as good. And I don't intend to touch *Your First Flight: A Night Flyer's Handbook (The Complete & Unabridged Version, Newly Updated!)* ever again.

How am I going to do nothing for two weeks? After a few days, I can't stand the boredom.

At the end of my first week, I go outside to take Cassie for a walk and step into a pile of snow. When did that happen? I have a momentary panic that I've done a Rip Van Winkle and slept for weeks or something, but a quick check of the calendar says it's December 4th. Normal enough date for snow, I guess. I walk and wonder why schools suspend people for protecting themselves. Shelley clearly started it, and I wasn't fighting back. I was just trying not to get killed.

What was I supposed to do? Let her annihilate me?

I drag my feet through the snow, and Cassie ambles along beside me. When I get back to my house, two people are standing at the doorstep.

One is Martin with an armload of paper.

The other is Everton.

Martin raises his hand when he sees me, but Everton doesn't budge. I guess my mother and the twins are out, or why would they both be shivering in the snow on the doorstep?

Martin calls out, "Hi, Gwen!"

"Hey," I say. "I'm really not in the mood for company." That sounds ruder than I intended.

"Well, here's your science homework. I went around to your other teachers and got their work for the week, too. You might as well not fall too far behind, right?"

"Thanks, Martin." I take the huge pile of papers from him.

"I can tutor you anytime. You didn't call." He says this with a quick look at Everton, who still hasn't said anything. "You should. Call. I can help."

Cassie licks his hand, and he has no more to say, so he says goodbye and then walks down the snowy street with his hands jammed in his coat.

"Can I help you?" I ask Everton, who is like a tall, dark brick in the wall.

"Do you want to go for a drive?"

"You can drive?" I ask, surprised. "Where to?"

He rubs his shoulders against the wall he's been holding up.

"A place I like."

I hesitate for a second.

"What about ... Abilith," I say, dropping my voice.

"Celestine and a friend." Everton points over his shoulder. I notice two shimmers of golden light on the roof that grow and shrink. For a second the shimmers turn into Celestine and another Spirit Flyer who looks very solemn and frankly a bit angry, like he'd rather not be here.

"Hi, Celestine," I say feeling very, very strange about talking to a Spirit Flyer chaperone at my front door. But the thought of getting out of my house and doing something with another human does appeal.

Hello, little golden sister. The Rogue is being hunted across the galaxy by my brothers and sisters. I will know if he is near. And I shall protect you.

"Thank you, Celestine," I say in my most polite voice. Part of me wants to point out that the last time I thought she was protecting me, I got swept away by the Rogue. But to be fair, I'm still not sure she was there that night. She's very obviously here now, plus there's the angry-looking Spirit Flyer, too.

"Okay, Everton, let's go."

I take Cassie into the house and feed her. I leave a note for my mom that I'm with Everton on a drive and won't be late (I don't mention Celestine, although I briefly consider it). If she wants to keep in constant contact with me, she should get me a phone. Everton stands slumped on the mat at the front door with his hands jammed in his pockets until I'm ready.

He leads me through the snow to the sidewalk and to his "car," which is a car only in name. It looks like a tin can on wheels. I've never seen this kind of car before.

"What is this?" I ask, backing away.

"My car. It's really old. My brother keeps it running. It passed the safety inspection. Barely." He grins.

"If you're old enough to drive, why are you in grade ten?" I ask to avoid getting in the car for as long as possible.

He shrugs. "I failed grade five." He grins again, and I think, *Fine, Everton. Whatever.* I climb in and slam the door as hard as I can. It doesn't fall off — a good start.

"Does it have heat?"

He laughs and starts the engine, and we drive along the snowy streets to the edge of town. The car does have heat, and soon it's pretty cozy. It feels fantastic to be going somewhere and to know that Spirit Flyers will watch out for me somewhere in the heavens above. I fiddle with the radio until I find music and watch the headlights catch the snowbanks at the edge of the road. Everton hasn't said much. It's a cold early evening. Soon it'll be dark.

"Where are we going?" I ask after a little while, but he just smiles at me.

"You'll see. Mr. McGillies isn't getting better," he says, his eyes on the road. I nod.

"Thanks for telling me." I can't think about Mr. McGillies right now. The image of my dad's feet flying up into the Shade pops into my head. I stare out the window.

"And I broke up with Shelley, she thinks because of you. I probably mentioned you once too often." He looks over at me for a second.

"That was stupid," I say. "But it probably explains why she tried to kill me in gym class. I can thank you for my suspension in that case."

Everton smiles, and I grimly smile back.

We drive along slowly. Everton is a good driver, and I feel pretty comfortable in his tin-can-on-wheels. We don't talk much, and after about an hour we turn off the highway into a parking lot with a sign that that says, "SCENIC LOOKOUT."

I can see why he likes this spot.

We park at the edge of the enormous lake. Beside us is the black water. The ice at the shore has formed into hills and pointed mountains that look like an alien landscape. The stars are bright up in the dark sky. I see a flutter of white feathers. Celestine shows herself for a second, perched like a statue on a nearby bank of snow, and then she vanishes to a gentle golden glimmer. A second golden glimmer lands beside her.

Off in the distance is the big city like a necklace of pearls, all lit up and glowing along the shore.

It's incredibly beautiful.

"The city looks a little like Mr. McGillies's bottle garden," I say, and Everton nods. We watch the far-off city for a long time. Everton keeps the car running and the heater on for a while, and we talk. I realize that I've missed talking to humans this week. Cassie hardly counts, and as much as I love Jez, she did all the talking and I did all the lying.

At first Everton talks about his life in the city.

"I've never met another Night Flyer even close to my age before," he says. This surprises me.

"Really? I'm the first?" He nods.

"It was pretty lonely in the city, actually, just me and thousands of other teenagers, and I was the only Night Flyer. I wanted to fly so badly all the time, but Emerson wouldn't let me. It's not like here. There are people everywhere in the city. There was nowhere safe to fly. You're lucky."

It just never occurred to me that there might be a reason I was lucky to live in a small town. I do have to be careful when I fly, but so far no one's ever seen me.

"I think it's one of the reasons I fought so much in school. I got kicked out of high school for fighting."

"YOU were suspended?"

He nods. "At first, yes. Then when I couldn't stop fighting, I got expelled. Out. Gone forever."

"They can do that?" I ask, a little shocked.

"Yep, I just moved from one school to the next until I ran out of schools. I couldn't stop fighting. It's actually pretty hard to stop once you start. That's why we're here in your lovely town. Well, one of the reasons." He plays with the radio for a minute, but he can't find the station he wants, so he leaves it and goes on.

"I haven't fought with anyone here so far. It's a new record for me. But maybe you'll be the fighter for the Night Flying community for a while?" He says this with such good humour that I smile and shake my head.

"It's not my fault! Shelley started it!"

"I'm sure she did. There's quite a bit about her you don't know."

"Like what?"

"I guess you're going to find out sooner or later. After your fight and the school got a little more involved in her family's business, the principal called Children's Aid. Shelley's living at a group home for a while until they find a foster home."

"What's wrong with her family?"

"Her dad beats her up. Stuff like that." I see Shelley's face and frown. No wonder she's always so mean.

Then we talk more about the city, and after a while I talk about me. I tell him about C2, I tell him a little about Martin (everything except the Worst Kiss Ever), and then I feel so calm that I tell him more.

"The Rogue showed me my dad."

I wasn't expecting to blurt this out. I look straight ahead at the fairy lights of the city, over at the snowbank glimmer that is Celestine and friend, and I know I can't stop now.

Drip.

A tear leaks onto my cheek. Then another.

Drip.

"He did?" Everton asks gently. He reaches into the back seat, cracks a bottle of water out of a case, and hands it to me.

"Thanks." I take a sip.

"So. What's he like? Abilith?"

I think about this. It's hard to focus on his face, on his manner. It's tough to answer.

"He's scary, but appealing in a weird way. I can't really describe him. I saw him in two ways, as a black figure with golden eyes and wings, and as a normal-looking man with weird green eyes. He looked a little like Mr. Tupperman."

Drip.

"And what did he show you?" he asks as gently as ever. I swallow hard. This isn't going to be easy. I take a deep breath and just say it.

Drip.

"He showed me ... my dad. In a storm. He went out to make sure a neighbour was okay." I can barely say the next part. "It was Mr. McGillies. Dad found Mr. McGillies, and they struggled back to the cabin." I hang my head, and both eyes are leaking now.

Drip. Drip. Drip.

"Then the Shade came. I saw the moment my dad died." My voice is so tiny, I'm not sure Everton hears that last part. But he must have, because he leans back in his seat and whispers solemnly, "No."

Then my faucet opens all the way. I start to really cry, and it's like every time I've cried in my life was just a practice for this performance.

But Everton doesn't stop me. I'm crying so hard that snot runs down my face (something that Jez would never allow if she were here), and I have no idea how long I cry. Everton sits and listens. After a while, he reaches into the back seat, pulls out a box of tissue from a big package (he must have just shopped at the bulk store or something), and opens it for me. I blow my nose, and eventually the faucet stops, and I'm exhausted and hiccupping.

I lean my head back against the seat.

I have no secrets from this boy now. He's seen me at my very worst, with my faucet full and broken and snot all over my face. And yet he's still here, warm and breathing and looking at me.

"Why didn't you tell me to *(hic)* stop? Why did you let me *(hic)* cry so hard?"

He leans sideways against the window, shifting in his seat a little, and considers me.

"You never asked me about my family, Gwen. Have you seen any parents at Miles Motors?" I take this in. No. No, I haven't. Everton lives with his brother.

He drops his voice and looks out the car window. The hair on the back of my neck starts to prickle. I don't think I want to hear what he's going to say.

"One night when I was in grade five, my parents were driving home from the Midsummer Party. They never liked to fly into the city because of all the people." Everton stops, then he whispers the next words. "A drunk driver hit them, somewhere near this spot. Killed them instantly. Emerson was old enough to take care of me, and he's been my legal guardian ever since." Everton takes a moment to look out the window. "That's right around the time I started fighting at school."

He looks solemn but calm, and this time I don't think *What charm*.

No. The words that come to mind this time are *I'm so sorry*.

I don't know what to say, but words maybe aren't important right now. We don't talk much on the drive home. We listen to music and I quietly watch the snow-covered hills. It starts to snow, and the windshield wipers squeal as they clear away the fast-falling flakes.

It's warm in the car, and once in a while I catch the shimmer of a Spirit Flyer in the snowbanks, following us high above.

I fall asleep, the deepest sleep I've had in a while. When we get to my house, a strong pair of arms helps me upstairs, and Everton's whisper brushes my cheek. "Goodnight, sweet Gwendolyn Golden."

But maybe that last part was just a dream.

TWENTY-SEVEN

Every night for the rest of my suspension, I stand at my window, longing to zoom over the trees. But even with Celestine and her friends nearby, I'm still too afraid to try. Instead, in the daytime I get out of the house as much as I can and walk.

On Tuesday of the second week, I get home after a whole day sitting in the window and sipping tea at The Float Boat. My mother is waiting for me, and as soon as I get in the door she hands me a letter. I snap it open. She's already read it, since the seal is broken. My name is very clearly on the envelope, but there's no point fighting about this. It's done, and there's a fight coming anyway. I can tell by the look on her face.

The letter is from the school board.

To the parent/guardian of Gwendolyn Imogen Golden,

As advised by Mr. Morton Skinty, principal of Bass Creek High School, your child/ward has been caught fighting with another student on school property. The school board requires as a condition of return to school that your child/ ward begins TWO sessions of therapy with a board-appointed and trained child psychologist at your expense. The first session must be completed before your child/ward returns to school....

There's more, but I skip to the bottom, which lists the phone numbers of the local child psychologist, and there's only one: Dr. Adam Parks.

I drop the letter onto the kitchen table and stare out the back door. Cassie takes one look at me and clears out into the living room. I cross my arms, and I can't bring myself to look at my mother, but when I do turn around, her face is unreadable. She does a good job trying not to look triumphant, or gleeful, or even compassionate. But I'm furious.

And this starts the biggest, loudest fight my mother and I have ever had.

We aren't very good at it.

"I'M NOT GOING!"

"You have to go if you want to go back to school." As soon as she says this, my mother realizes she has made a tactical error. I laugh at her.

"AS IF I CARE ABOUT GOING BACK TO SCHOOL!"

We carry on like this for a while until my mother says, "Gwen, you have to go. You have no choice. I can see that you're afraid of Dr. Parks for some reason. You don't want to talk about your dad?"

That's the last straw for me. In slow motion, I pick up a teacup from the table and smash it at my feet without taking my eyes off my mother. She swallows but doesn't look away. This is the first time china has been smashed in our house, as far as I know. I've crossed a line, and I'm not all that sure how to get back.

I grab my coat and storm out the front door. It feels good to slam it behind me, but it's an empty gesture, the cup smashing and the door slamming.

I've lost. I have to go to see Dr. Adam Parks.

Angry tears blind me for a while, and that night I stay out as long as I can. I walk all around town. It's snowy and cold, but it doesn't drive me indoors. I drift past The Float Boat and then past Miles Motors. Both places are lit up, friends are inside, and I could go and talk to them.

I could. But I don't.

Eventually I end up back at home. I sneak up to my room, but my mom calls out hello as I close my bedroom door. I don't answer her.

Instead I sit and read *Your First Flight: A Night Flyer's Handbook (The Complete & Unabridged Version, Newly Updated!)* until the sky gets pink and clear in the east. I start at the beginning, and by the time I fall asleep I've read more than three hundred pages. I finish the first five chapters: *History and Hysteria (Prehistory to 1454), The Burning Time (Our Darkest Hour, 16th century), The Grand Council of Night Flyers (1718–1789), Night Flyers in* the Early Industrial Age (1800–1880), and *Colonial Flyers From Pole to Pole (1885–1913)*. I can't say I understand much of it, but the pictures help, and I fall asleep with a lot of history swirling around in my head. This is my history, this is my tribe, if I choose this life for all time at the Midsummer Party.

Do I *want* to be a Night Flyer forever?

It's a choice I have to make, and I don't want to.

That's one thing you can do when you're suspended from the activities of normal life; your timeline isn't like anyone else's. You can stay up until 5:00 a.m. reading about your alternate life, your legendary self, the possibilities for your future, and no one cares.

The next day, when I go down to the kitchen after Mom and the twins have left for the day, there's a note on the calendar.

My first appointment with Dr. Adam Parks is on Friday, my last day of suspension. My eyes fill with angry tears again, but there's nothing I can do. I slam around the kitchen and make myself lunch, I take Cassie for a quick walk, and then I head back to the library, where I lose myself in an afternoon of reading.

I'm so engrossed (I'm reading *The Adventures of Huckleberry Finn* again) that I hardly notice when the library starts to get busy with after-school kids. I also don't notice when a person stands in front of me and clears their throat. Twice.

Finally I do notice and look up.

Martin stands in front of me. "Hi, can I sit down?"

I wave my hand at a chair, and he drops into it.

He looks bigger, more substantial, but maybe it's his huge winter coat. He pulls a bunch of paper out of his backpack, followed by our science textbook.

"Planets this week. You should start reading. I can help." He shoves the book at me, and I groan.

"Thanks, Martin, but not today." He looks crestfallen.

"Okay, I tell you what. We'll start tutoring next week. Really, Martin, I appreciate the help."

"Okay, next week." He grins a little, then he clears his throat. He's not finished.

"What?"

"I thought I should tell you, I actually came looking for you to tell you, and Jez said you'd be here. Mr. McGillies is in the hospital." I don't think my face changes at all, but my stomach drops at the name.

"It's mostly for tests," he adds quickly. "I think he should be home by next week. I'm going to visit him tomorrow. Do you want to come?"

"No, no thanks. Maybe some other time." How could I possibly go and visit Mr. McGillies in the hospital, knowing what I know? But since we're on the topic of Mr. McGillies, I see my chance to do a little probing.

"Why do you do so much for him, Martin? Why do you care what happens to him?"

Martin shrugs. "We're friends. I used to play chess with him here on Saturdays when I was a kid. My mom would dump me at the library all day so she could go shopping or meet with her knitting group or whatever, and I'd get lonely sitting here for hours. Mr. McGillies was always here too, and one afternoon he taught me checkers, then after a while we started playing chess. For years I came to the library every weekend to lose at that chess table right there." Martin points over at a table where two old men are intently bent over chess pieces.

"Mr. McGillies is a fantastic chess player, bet you didn't know that. I heard from one of the librarians that he was a national champion once when he was young. I really looked forward to our chess games, then we had to stop last summer because he got sick."

First Miss Moreau tells me Mr. McGillies was a famous artist and taught art classes to kids, and now Martin says he was a national chess champion?

Martin looks a little sad then says, "I hope he gets to go back and sit in the bottle garden when the summer comes." He doesn't say, "If he lives that long."

But he's thinking it. We both are.

We change the subject and talk about school and Mr. Tupperman, then Martin gets out his phone and calls Jez (because I know her number) and Everton (because he knows Everton's number). My friends, our friends, come and join us at the library for a while. Then we drift over to The Float Boat and talk and eat until Mrs. Forest gently tells us she's going to bed. After that, we move on to Miles Motors down the street. The four of us sit in the mechanic shop window with a table and a candle and talk for hours. Martin and Everton are polite enough not to talk about Abilith and what happened out at the cabin, so my lying to Jez never comes up, although I feel bad about it. It's clearer and clearer that I have to tell her the truth, soon. I will. First chance I get.

But for tonight, we're just four normal teenagers talking. It's really late by the time Everton and Martin walk Jez and me home. I tease them that they have to get up for school, but I don't.

Hanging out with my oldest friend Jez, friending Everton, and re-friending Martin isn't that hard.

Therapy, though, that's going to be much, much harder.

TWENTY-EIGHT

I have to go to my first therapy session any minute.

My mother and I have managed an uneasy truce. I apologize for breaking the teacup (although I hate to admit how long it takes me), and she is kind enough about it, although it was her favourite.

"You have a bad temper, Gwendolyn, and so did your dad. I know you don't want to talk about him, but you may actually find that it helps once you get to know Adam … Dr. Parks … a little."

So this morning before she leaves the house, I ask Mom what Dr. Adam Parks does with C2 for an hour every week. Her answer is not reassuring.

"They colour pictures and form clay. They make crazy worlds out of trains and figures, or dance around the room to cool drum music." I have no idea what my face does when she tells me this, but she bursts out laughing.

"*What*?" Drum music?

"Don't worry, Gwen, I'm pretty sure he won't be asking you to dance around." Then she gets serious.

"I know you don't want to go. But lots of people go to therapy, families, kids, adults. You can say whatever you want, and I never have to know what you say to him, unless you want to tell me. This is about you Gwen, no one else, it's a chance to tell someone how you feel about things."

I scowl. How dare she assume I feel anything at all?

She takes my hand. "I'm sorry I can't come with you, but I can't take any more time off work. Will you be okay? Take Jez for moral support."

I nod. I shrug. I'm pleased that my mother has forgiven me for breaking the cup, and she isn't giving me a hard time about getting suspended or the fact that she has to pay for the therapy (it's not cheap), so I can't get too mad at her. She squeezes my hand, and for a second I squeeze back, then she has to go to work.

After school, Jez comes by my house, and we walk together to the clinic. I've decided that my body can show up since it has to, but that doesn't mean I'm going to be there.

We walk along the busy streets. There are only a few weeks left before the winter holiday, and people drive through town with Christmas trees tied to their cars. Holiday music belts out from the stores, and when we pass the library, the people who run the homeless shelter are out front collecting for the poor. The grocery store parking lot is jammed.

Jez chats away with her arm linked through mine. She tells me about the date she went on with the short boy from her math class, Prentice some-body. *What a weird name*, I think. We get closer and closer to the clinic, and I'm more and more nervous. Finally, I can't stand it another second.

"Look, Jez, there's something I haven't told you." I look into my friend's eyes, and I feel suddenly very sad that I haven't told her about the Rogue. Odd that I chose to tell Everton the truth instead of her. Even Martin knows more than she does.

"Is it about Everton?" she asks.

"Kind of. It's more about the Night Flyers around here, and something else. Something bad." She looks bewildered.

"What does that mean? Are you in trouble, Gwen?" Jez is so up-front, her face is so open. No more lies, so I just tell her. I tell her about Abilith, about Everton, about the bottle garden and Martin. I even tell her about Celestine. I tell her everything except what Abilith showed me. For some reason Everton is the only one I want to share that with. And as we walk along the slippery sidewalk, she just listens. She hears me out, until suddenly we find ourselves in front of the clinic.

"I'm sorry I didn't tell you sooner," I mumble. She sighs and looks at me with a flash of something, dis-appointment and sadness more than anger, I think. I've never seen that look on my best friend's face before, and I hope I never do again. She's quiet for a moment then speaks with the greatest dignity, like a queen.

"That sounds horrifying, but I'm not going to pretend I'm not hurt. You used to tell me everything."

It's the closest Jez has ever come to getting mad at me. She looks puzzled and sad. I mumble sorry again, then Jez gives me a hug, and that's that. The truth is out. Most of it, anyway.

"Do you want me to stay?" she asks, looking up at the clinic stairs. I know that she would. Despite everything, she'll wait on hard, bum-rotting chairs if I ever need her to.

I smile. "No. Thanks, though." She heads down the street and tells me to call her when I get home. I register with the lady at the desk and then, before I can sit down, Dr. Adam Parks calls me into his office.

I walk in, and there's no drum music playing, or none that I can detect. I perch in an overstuffed armchair next to the door, and he sits on the other side of the round table, which I notice he's cleared of blocks and snap-together toys. The only things on the table are a thick pad of paper and a few pens.

"Well, this probably isn't the way you were expecting to meet again, is it?" he says when we're settled.

"No." Monosyllables. That'll work. Here in body only.

He pauses.

"Gwendolyn, in here you can talk about anything, it doesn't have to be about fighting at school. We can talk about music. Snow. Friends. Books. It's up to you."

I must perk up at the word "books," because next he says, "Books then?" He gets up and strides over to a bookcase against the wall, reaching high and low, and comes back with four books.

The first two are romance stories I wouldn't touch with a pool pole. He shows me the covers, then judges my look and says, "Okay, no. What about these?"

He drops a book on the table. *The Adventures of Huckleberry Finn*.

Then he drops another. *A Wrinkle in Time*.

I stare at the cover of *Huckleberry Finn*. How odd. I had a library copy of this book in my backpack the first time I came in here, but he didn't see it. I haven't stopped reading it since. The cover of this copy is interesting. It has a boy and a man on a raft, floating down a wide river at sunset. The cover of *A Wrinkle in Time* has a winged centaur creature flying around some very tall, icy mountains, which is also intriguing. This book has been on my mental "to-be-read" list for a while.

Well played, Dr. Adam Parks.

"I'll start with *Huckleberry Finn*," I say. He goes to his desk and puts on some soft music, which doesn't appear to have any drums, it's mostly guitar.

"Why don't you read for a few minutes, then we'll talk about the book." Then he sits and reads his own book, which is something about child psychology. It's almost as thick as the *Night Flyer's Handbook*. I open the first page of *Huckleberry Finn*. It has "Adam Parks" scrawled on it in youngish writing, like he couldn't have been more than about ten when he wrote it.

Then I start to read. I've already read this book cover-to-cover twice, but he doesn't need to know that. Huck isn't like anyone else. If he were around today, he'd be a ward of the state, living in foster homes without anyone who really understood him. Although I might.

I'm at the part where Huck's no-good dad is paddling across the water fully intending to kill him, a part that always worried me, when Dr. Adam Parks stands up and says, "Time's up, Gwendolyn. Actually, it was up about five minutes ago. I didn't want to stop you."

It's so jarring to have to stop when you're right in the middle of a great sentence that I finish reading the page before I look up. My face is flushed, and I think he can tell that my heart is pounding.

"What's going on with Huck?" he asks, taking a seat across the table.

"He's got a crazy dad."

"He does." There's a long silence, so I look up at the ceiling and listen to the gentle guitar music.

"He'll be okay, though," I say after what seems like far too much silence. I want to wait Dr. Adam Parks out, but he's good at sitting still. Better than me.

"That's an interesting thought. Does he seem like anyone you know?"

For the strangest reason, Shelley Norman's face flashes into my head.

"Maybe?" I say this hopefully. I've never been that great in English class, and I'm not used to talking about books. To my relief, Dr. Adam Parks nods.

"Books can remind us of people we know. I think that's what makes a book a classic. We may even see ourselves." This hits me hard. Huck floats downriver with Jim, just like Everton and I float over our town. Huck's dad dies. Everton and I know what that's like. He's right. I do see someone I know in Huck.

Then we really start to talk about books. About my favourites (the boy wizard books — I leave out Huckleberry Finn for now), about what scenes I like best (scenes of flying, not surprisingly, although I don't tell him why, of course), and what I don't like (the family scenes, when the boy wizard misses his parents). Dr. Adam Parks and I talk for what seems like a few minutes, but then I realize is over an hour.

At some point he stands up and says we'll have to continue the conversation next week. I put *The Adventures of Huckleberry Finn* on the table, and Dr. Adam Parks says, "Take it with you, Gwendolyn."

"I've already read it twice."

He raises an eyebrow and says, "Okay, take this one then." He offers me *A Wrinkle in Time*, but that winged centaur on the cover has me weirded out.

"Thanks, but I'm not really interested in a fantasy about flying creatures at the moment."

"Okay, no books this week."

"Thanks, Doctor," I say.

"It's Adam. Just Adam. See you same time next week." Then he shuts the door, and I run all the way home.

Therapy session #1 survived.

TWENTY-NINE

It's Saturday night, and I'm in bed, flipping through the first few chapters of the *Night Flyer's Handbook*. Those T. Bosch drawings call me, and I study them carefully. *The Monster Meets Her End. The Misfortunes of the Night Flying Monster.* I've carefully avoided the picture of the *Rogue Spirit Flyer, Abilith, as described to T. Bosch*, though.

There's a sudden, insistent *tap, tap, tap!* at my window.

I jump.

Get a grip on yourself! Abilith wouldn't knock!

I tiptoe carefully across the room and peek outside.

It's Everton. He's wearing a lumberjack coat and a flap-eared hat, and he looks so hilarious floating there in workboots and a coat that I laugh. I open the window.

"Everton, what are you doing?"

"Come on, get your stuff on, you want to see this." I'm standing in a flannel nightgown.

"See what?"

"It's a full moon, and you want to see this. I want to take you to Mr. McGillies's cabin."

"What? Are you crazy? No way!" I go to slam the window, and he stops me.

"Gwendolyn, I promise it's safe. But I asked Celestine to bring backup." He looks over his shoulder, and Celestine and two Spirit Flyers float patiently beside the neighbour's house. They look distant but mighty. Their whiteness is blinding, and each one carries feathers across their shoulders like hers, but theirs are bigger, brighter, and brilliant white. She really does look young next to her older brothers and sisters.

Celestine raises her hand. I raise mine back.

Greetings, Gwendolyn Golden.

"It's such a beautiful night, you don't want to miss this. You'll be totally safe. The Rogue is nowhere near us. I promise," Everton says, and it's all too irresistible.

I've been dying to fly for weeks, but I've been too scared. I hesitate a moment longer, but the look on Everton's face is so infectious that I can't fight it. I close the window, throw on long johns, warm jeans, and a sweater, then I tiptoe downstairs and grab my down-filled jacket and my boots. I'm back upstairs and out the window in seconds.

Everton's right, it's a gorgeous night. The moon is huge in a coal-black, eternal sky.

We float past the Spirit Flyers, gracious and noble, large and bright. They fill me with warmth, and Celestine's voice fills my head.

Welcome to the wintery night, little golden sister. You are safe from the Rogue, do not fear. My brothers and sisters tell me that he is far, far from here. Come, fly.

Everton and I take off over the sleeping, snowy town. The moon is so bright and huge overhead, making every snow-covered hill and tree flash with a million tiny stars of light. The Spirit Flyers are high above us almost out of sight, but I can feel them there. If I look hard enough, I think I can see them, starshot immortals keeping us safe, tracking us like satellites.

We pick up speed at the outskirts of town, and I'm so joyful to be flying again. It feels so, so good, even if I am wearing a down-filled coat and winter boots. It's nothing like flying in the summer. I have a brief thought that it would be an advantage to be a Night Flyer somewhere warm like Hawaii. It really would.

Soon we see Mr. McGillies's cabin in the distance, and I get a shiver of fear. Everton notices and comes closer to my side, and we fly quickly. As soon as I feel fear the Spirit Flyers drop into sight and my fears vanish.

There's no light on in the cabin for the first time I can remember.

"Close your eyes," Everton demands as we get closer. He takes my hand, and we descend slowly until my boots crunch on snow.

"Open them."

I open my eyes and gasp. The moonlight reflects off the snow and ice-covered bottle garden. It looks like fairyland, and a breeze makes the bottle bushes gently ring.

"The moon really makes it glow," Everton says, pleased.

It's the most beautiful sight I've ever seen. I can't tear my eyes away.

"Like it?"

"How could I not like it? It's beautiful."

We sit on one of the glass benches, and Everton pulls out a flask.

He pours liquid into the lid. "It's hot chocolate. I made it." We sip hot chocolate and watch the moon cross the sky. We talk about school and about our friends. I tell him about therapy and Dr. Adam Parks, I even tell him about Huckleberry Finn. He tells me he went to therapy a few times after his parents died, but he hated the therapist, so he stopped going.

And then we talk about growing up missing someone we love. It's not that hard to talk to Everton. It's weird having the place to ourselves, and I'm still a little nervous that Abilith is going to appear, but I also know that he won't. I'm a bit sad when Everton tells me that Mr. McGillies has been moved into town to stay in the men's shelter. He's out of the hospital, though, at least for now. I guess his doctors decided he needed more constant help, and the cabin is too cold for a sick old man. I'm sad that he can't be here to see how beautiful his bottles are in the moonlight, but we're here, Everton and I, to see it for him.

I'll describe it to him if I ever see him again.

The Spirit Flyers stand motionless and gently golden against the snowy fields the entire time.

THIRTY

The first week back at school is a weird blessing. No one seems to notice my absence. It's like I was hardly away. People have short memories, I guess, or I'm just not that interesting. Either way, it's okay to walk the halls again and have no one pay attention to me. I go to science with Martin, I go to pottery class with Jez, I even go to gym, and Shelley Norman completely ignores me.

School has been transformed in my absence. Holiday decorations cover the walls and windows, and a food drive box overflows in front of the principal's office.

The week zooms by, but I've missed quite a bit despite Martin's kind efforts. I'm ashamed to admit that I never did do any of the homework he brought me.

Then on Friday I have my second therapy appointment with Dr. Adam Parks. Adam. As I'm sitting there with my bum turning to stone on the hard plastic chair, the office door opens and Jeffrey

Parks walks out. He mumbles, "Hi, Gwendolyn," and brushes past me.

"Hi, Jeffrey," I mumble back. Then Jeffrey slides out the clinic door without a sound.

Adam comes out of his office and calls my name and says hello. I follow him inside, and today there IS drum music playing. It's actually good, and I'm disappointed when he turns it off and sits down across from me. On the table between us is a child's drawing. Adam sees me looking.

"Christine drew that last week. She left it for you."

I pick it up and look closely at my sister's art. A girl that looks like Christine floats above a field of flowers. I notice there's no Christopher in the picture. I think I might look a bit worried.

"Your sister has a vivid imagination, don't you think? She has dreams about flying. Did you know that? It's not unusual for kids her age." I know I look worried now.

"She dreams that your dad could fly, too," he says, very quietly.

My heart leaps. Then my eyes sting.

Drip.

A tear rolls down my cheek.

"I'm not sure I can talk about my dad," I whisper. *Please don't make me!*

"You have real memories of him. Christine doesn't, so she dreams about him. It's natural."

Drip ... d ... drip.

I struggle for something safe to say, something that has nothing to do with me or my family.

"Huckleberry had a terrible dad," I manage.

"That's true," Adam says gently. "Nothing like yours. From what I hear, he was a great dad."

Drip. D … d … drip. Drip.

There goes the faucet. For a horrible second, the tap opens and this sound comes out of me. It's a little kid sound, a sound a six-year-old might make. A hoot, a cry, and a sob (something I don't remember actually doing when I was six), all mixed together with tears.

I'm pretty sure this is what I've been afraid of.

First Everton's car. Now here. Once you start to feel things, it's hard to stop.

Adam says kindly, "Take a breath, Gwendolyn." Which I do. Clearly he's no stranger to leaky faucets, since he knows exactly when to hand me the tissues. My tears stop fast, but I clutch the box of tissues like they'll protect me. Like a little kid. Adam leans back in his chair.

"You may not think so, but you're a great big sister. The twins never stop talking about you. If they were here and you could tell them anything about your dad, what would you say?" he asks.

And that's it. I just start talking. I go from crying to chatting in about two minutes, which feels a little crazy, honestly, but it's like a light switches on. I talk and talk about my father, everything that I can remember, anyway, the funny things we did, the places we liked, moments that I can remember as clear as a bell, even though I've hidden them away for years because it just hurt too much.

It's odd but the more I talk, the more I remember. It's a flood of memories, not tears this time, though, which is a nice change. Adam asks a few questions, but mostly he just listens and I talk.

Finally I get up to leave. "Come back any time, Gwendolyn. I'm here except next week, when I'm taking my nephew to Florida," he says.

A penny drops. "Jeffrey Parks. Jeffrey's your nephew." He nods. I'm suddenly glad that sad Jeffrey has someone to talk to. Come to think of it, he hasn't cried again in school since the first day.

"Have a good holiday. Keep reading the classics," Adam says then locks the clinic door behind me. I walk home thinking about Christine and her drawing. Did I dream about flying when I was her age? Before I could actually fly. I can't remember.

It's dark out when I get home. My two school-appointed sessions are over. Good thing, since the whole Night Flyer part of my life was getting awfully close to the surface.

I feel my father's feather next to my heart, and I'm tired but lighter, much lighter all the way home. Almost light enough to float away.

THIRTY-ONE

The last few days of school before the winter holiday go by in a blur.

We're doing square dance in gym, which is just ridiculous. Why would anyone want teenagers to square dance? Shelley Norman keeps a wide berth and laughs with her friends. They aren't laughing at me, which is a nice change. There's a new cleanliness to her, too, which I have to say isn't all that bad.

Then I score a major success in our last pottery class.

I still haven't created a leak-free goblet. The first few goblets created a flood. After a while, I managed to get the flood down to a few drops. Last week the goblet almost held, and just a tiny bead of moisture rolled out of the bottom. Every time I show my work to Chas, it leaks and he says, "Next week, Gwendolyn." I have no idea if he actually expects my goblet ever to hold water. I know I don't.

But today, we take my dried goblet out of the kiln and I hold it like a fragile little bird. Everyone goes up with their creation and quietly talks it over with Chas, then one by one they leave the class as he wishes them a happy holiday. Then it's Jez's turn, and her creation is a fantastic bowl with curly handles like something you'd find in a Greek exhibit at the museum. It's perfect, like every week.

Then it's my turn. I cautiously take my goblet up to the front of the class, and we pour water into it and wait patiently. Then we wait a little longer, and a little longer. Since I've never created a goblet that doesn't leak, I have no idea how long we have to wait.

Ten seconds. Twenty. Thirty. And Chas says, "Congratulations, Gwendolyn, you're holding water! Happy holidays!" This feels like a major victory for some reason. I stow Shelley Norman's smock on my peg and head out into the hall with my water-retaining clay goblet. Down the hall, I see Everton laughing with Martin at his locker.

Everton calls me over. I join them with my goblet clutched in my hands.

"Did you win something? The House Cup for Hufflepuff?" Everton teases me.

"No. It doesn't leak," I answer, which makes them both burst out laughing.

Whatever. I roll my eyes, but Everton doesn't let me get too mad. He puts his hand on my arm for a second, then drops it.

"I have to go to the city for the holidays. I'm staying with my aunt, but I'll come over as soon as I get back." He drops his voice. "If you fly, call *her*." For a moment he's very close to me. I can feel his heat, smell the scent of his shampoo. He smiles, those dark blue eyes shine, and he whispers, "Be good, Gwendolyn Golden."

I walk away cradling my cup, my heart beating a little too hard, my cheeks oddly flushed.

In our last science class together for the term, Martin and I are friendly and chatty. His tutoring really helped. He's so helpful, in fact, that when Mr. Tupperman hands us our last test, Martin and I are gleeful over the red *68%, much better!* scrawled at the top of the page. As we gather our books and get up to leave, Martin slips me an envelope.

"Open it later," he says quietly. "Have a great holiday, Gwen. Call if you want to do anything, like go to a movie or something," he says, then he's gone.

I stuff the letter into my backpack and forget about it.

At the very end of the day we have a holiday assembly which everyone fidgets through. Then Jez and I walk C2 home through the snowy streets, and after I feed them and stick them in front of the television to watch holiday specials, Jez and I hide out in my bedroom. I pull some books out of my bag, and Martin's card falls out. Jez grabs it, teasing me.

"What's this?"

I groan. "Oh, don't open it. It's from Martin." Something about the way he looked at me when he told me to "open it later" has me worried.

Jez ignores me and rips it open. It's a Christmas card with sparkles on it. Santa stands on a rooftop with the moon behind him. He's got his arm around a red-nosed reindeer. Inside it says, *You're my Rudolph, friends for life! Happy Holidays.*

It's signed Martin E. A single *x* stands on a line of its own below his name.

Jez seems a little surprised. I'm mortified.

"A kiss? Whoa," she says. We both stare at it until I groan and grab the card and smash it closed.

That little *x* makes me blush. Since he started tutoring me, there's been no more tension about holding hands or anything like that. We get along great as friends, so the thought of an *x* makes me break out in a sweat. Although he did apologize for the terrible *x* last summer, is he hoping there are more *x*'s in our future?

I jam the card under my bed with my handbook. Jez is no help.

"He really likes you, Gwen. He always did."

A few months ago this might have made me happy. Martin is a nice guy, despite his horrible mother and the Worst Kiss Ever. But it's impossible to think about Martin in that way now.

A pair of dark blue eyes keep popping up whenever I try to think of Martin's face.

It's hopeless.

THIRTY-TWO

The holidays are different this year. For one thing, Mom has a little more money due to her promotion at work, which is new for us. We never have much money. That means that C2 get exactly what they asked for: matching rocket sleds.

My mom gives me a bookstore gift card and a really nice sweater. But my big gift? My first phone. Well, it's not entirely mine. I have to share it with my mom, which to me completely misses the point. How exactly am I supposed to contact her if she has the phone, and I'm out somewhere and want to call her? But at least we have one. It's a start.

I spend Christmas morning reading the instructions. There's quite a bit to know. I set it up with my mother's initials and mine, since we're sharing it: EGG.

My first text is to Jez. I've phoned her from home for years, so I know her number.

Sup?

I think this is funny, since she doesn't know I have a phone, or part of one. And what normal person would call herself EGG? She texts back *wrong number*, then *who is this*, then *stop*, and along that generally annoyed tone for a bit. Finally I text, *How's the short guy? What's his name? Prentice?* She texts back, *Gwen?*

Joke's over, but it was fun while it lasted. Then Jez and her mom go out of town for the rest of the holidays, and she's forbidden to text and has to turn off her phone. We have a quiet holiday dinner, just Mom, C2, Cassie, and me. Then after everyone is full of turkey, we lie down on the couch and the floor and play Monopoly. It's a new set that the twins got as a gift, since the old one is spread out all over the house.

Christine wins. Christopher spends an hour showing us his impression of his teacher and his schoolmates, which is hilarious, and Mom, Cassie, and I watch from the couch. I'm tired and calm, and I go to bed feeling almost normal.

I read the final few chapters of *Your First Flight: A Night Flyer's Handbook: Courage in the Skies (Allied Night Flyers behind the Lines 1914–1946), Enemies and Entities (A Beginner's Primer),* and finally *A Modernist View (Rules, Regulations, and Responsibilities, Prehistory to Present Day).*

The *Enemies and Entities* chapter I've already partly read (I skip the page with Abilith's picture on it). I could definitely tell the editors a thing or two on the subject of RSFs. I'm hardly a beginner there. I skim, but I do stop to read the section on the Shade.

It's a ridiculously short entry (and no illustration from T. Bosch, I notice): *A cloud of misery and despair, seeks to overcome the innocent or unsuspecting, typically in moments of great stress, exertion, or even delight. Populated with souls of the dead trapped by the sad memories of the living, escape is almost impossible. Avoid the Shade at all costs.*

The editors do have a gift for understatement. I try not to think about my father's feet or Mr. McGillies, and skip to the last chapter, *A Modernist View.* It's no fun either.

The Rules part is pretty simple. Basically there's only one: don't let non-flyers catch you flying, and if they do and want to burn you at the stake, you're on your own. (It's not the first time I think the *Night Flyer's Handbook* hasn't been as "newly updated!" as the editors pretend.)

The Regulations part is mostly about being a good Watcher or Mentor, if you ever take the oath to be one. Neither job sounds all that appealing, frankly. Just a lot of worry and late nights.

The Responsibilities section is most worrying of all, since it's pretty much all about the choice you have to make about your gift of flight, one year after your first Midsummer Party.

To fly or not to fly.

It's the last chapter. As I close the book, I realize I'm officially finished *Your First Flight: A Night Flyer's Handbook (The Complete & Unabridged Version, Newly Updated!)*, which is both a relief and leaves me oddly proud that I actually got through it. It's under my bed, where it's going to stay for a while. Something I won't dip into that often, but it'll always be there if I need it.

A few days before school starts, I'm sitting in the window of The Float Boat, sipping tea. I look out at the sleepy, snowy street when all the shoppers in the store suddenly leave and the place falls quiet. I've noticed that a store is like a beach; people come and go in waves.

Mrs. Forest joins me at the table with her own cup of tea. She blows on it, and a waft of mint drifts over to me.

"Mrs. Forest, what exactly are the Spirit Flyers?" Her eyebrows shoot up, because we haven't talked about Night Flying in ages.

"They're immortals, guardians. They keep an eye out for us. If you need one, any Spirit Flyer can show up."

"Need one?"

"Yes, if you need protection, or guarding, or help if you're in mortal danger, they'll appear if you call them. Usually."

I think about this. "Does everyone get a Spirit Flyer? Not just Night Flyers?"

She takes a sip of tea and shakes yes and no. "That I can't answer, honey. I can't say what guardians might watch other people. Far as I know, the Spirit Flyers are just for us, but they aren't the only good out there." I take a sip of my own tea.

"Why aren't they mentioned anywhere in the *Night Flyer's Handbook*?" Mrs. Forest looks surprised.

"They aren't?" I shake my head, and she shrugs. "Well, maybe it's because they wrote it."

I nod. Okay. Sure. It's weird enough to be written by starshot immortals. Why not? I'll have to ask more about that later, because right now I have a more important question.

"Mrs. Forest, why didn't the Spirit Flyers save my dad?" I say this really quietly. I can't look at her, so I stare out the window at the sidewalk. It's snowing a little now, and the afternoon sun goes behind a cloud. Mrs. Forest might have taken me in her arms even a few short months ago, but she can't now. I'm older. I'm wiser. I don't need a hug — I need answers.

"I don't know, Gwendolyn. I don't know why they keep an eye out for some of us but aren't there for others. Maybe they thought your dad could take care of himself, or maybe they were looking the other way when he called. They do have limits."

I'm about to ask her what she means when Martin walks in.

"Hey, Mrs. Forest. Hi, Gwendolyn!" Is he blushing? Or maybe his cheeks are just rosy from the cold outside. There's an old grocery cart on the porch of The Float Boat, half full of bottles. "Do you have any today, Mrs. Forest?"

"Two bags," she says. She disappears into the back room, returns with two bags filled with glass bottles, and hands them over to Martin.

"Thanks, see you next week, Mrs. Forest. Bye, Gwen," he says quickly. He's still blushing. Then he walks out to the porch and dumps the new bottles into the cart. That cart looks awfully familiar.

"Bye, Mrs. Forest!" I grab my coat and run outside. Martin is already heading down the sidewalk. He's about to stop at the bakery next door.

"Martin!" He stops and looks awkward.

"Hi, Gwen." He squints a little because the sun has come back out. He looks sweet standing there in the snow beside Mr. McGillies's old bottle cart.

"Thanks for my card, Martin, that was nice." Nice? Embarrassing, really, but I can't say that now, can I? It was the right thing to say, though, because he smiles and there's no doubt about it. Those cheeks aren't red because of the cold. He clearly can't think of a thing to say, so I help him out.

"Collecting bottles for the garden?"

He shakes his head. "No, while he's sick I'm carrying on what Mr. McGillies did every Saturday."

"What did he do?"

"He collected bottles then cashed them in and donated the money to the men's homeless shelter. You didn't know that?" I must look completely astonished. How did I not know that about Mr. McGillies? He's an artist, a champion chess player, and now I find out he's a doer of good deeds?

"I honestly thought he just hoarded all those bottles." I say this weakly, and frankly I'm now ashamed of myself. Clueless.

"Well, most of the time he did hoard them, except the bottles he collected on Saturdays. Do you want to help?" Martin asks brightly. "Of course I want to help," I say just as brightly, and we walk into the bakery together then back out with two more bags of donated bottles. We spend all afternoon collecting bottles up and down the main street, and by the time we cash the bottles in at the grocery store, we've earned $9.25. Martin takes me to the men's shelter, another place I've never been, and we hand the money to the man at the front desk.

"Thanks, Martin, see you next week!" the man calls.

Then Martin and I go to a movie. It's NOT a date, just two friends out to watch a movie together. When I call Jez, days later to tell her, she agrees it's just a friendly movie, because there are no x's involved.

Martin asked once, but I said no.

THIRTY-THREE

Winter term starts, and life really does return to normal. Everton is back, and it's great to see him. He stops me in the hall every time he sees me, and we chat. I have a popular older friend, a first for me. I've never been remotely popular.

For the first few weeks back at school, my life is pretty much taken up by trying a little harder at everything and taking care of C2.

Mom is really busy at work, and I have to pick them up every day after school, and get them fed and doing their homework. Once Adam's office opens again, I have to take them to therapy. It's fine, though. I just sit on the uncomfortable plastic chairs and do my homework for the hour.

Once in a while, the noise in Adam's office gets so loud and hilarious that the other people in the waiting room look a little worried, and I just smile. That's C2 in there, dancing to loud drum music, squealing, thumping, or basically being hooligans. And Dr. Adam Parks goes right along with them.

There are quiet periods too, though, where I think Adam gets them to draw or paint or build stuff. We already have a raft of pretty interesting art on the fridge. There are so many sheets under each magnet that they flutter to the floor if you slam the door too hard. There aren't any more pictures of Christine flying, I notice.

One day late in February while I'm waiting for them, the office outer door opens and a teenager walks in muffled in a coat and hat and then takes a seat across from me. When the hat comes off, I sneak a peek and gasp.

It's Shelley Norman.

I tense up. I'm shocked. But it occurs to me that if I was here doing two sessions for protecting myself, then she might have to do even more for actually starting a fight. Plus, there's the whole group home/foster care angle. We lock eyes, and I honestly want to bolt for the door. No one else is around, and even the receptionist isn't at her seat. I must look terrified.

Shelley curls her lip, but she doesn't lash out at me. Instead she says, "Don't worry, Golden. Adam wouldn't like us fighting in here."

"No, he wouldn't." I notice she has a healed cut on her lip.

"Sorry about your lip. Did I do that?" I actually am sorry, although I'm not sure if I'm responsible.

Shelley looks me in the eye. "That was months ago. What do you think?" Then she closes into herself and picks up a magazine. I listen to her breathing and don't say another word, but I'm thinking that if I didn't put that cut on Shelley's lip, then who did? Was it a last wallop from her father before she left for good?

Thankfully, a few moments later the door opens and my brother and sister burn out of Adam's office at a run. Then, like a one-minded creature, they both swerve back and give him a big hug, one on each side. Then they race past me and I have to run to catch them. I manage a backward, "Thank you, see you next week!"

"Today's their last session," Adam says.

"Oh! Okay ... thank you?" I sincerely hope my mother will eventually come and say thank you more thoroughly. I hope it's not another responsibility of hers I have to take on.

Who should thank a therapist for straightening out her children? A mother, not a fourteen-year-old sibling, I'm pretty sure. "I'll let my mother know?" I say with another question. I have to go, because C2 are marauding down the snowy street.

Adam says, "I'll phone her, don't worry. Bye, Gwendolyn."

As I leave, I hear Adam say, "Come on in, Shelley." Then he and Shelley disappear into his office.

As I run down the stairs, I realize that's my last visit to his office. Shelley never appeared in the office waiting room at the same time as me before, and a part of me wonders if Adam had us meet this one last time on purpose.

But what would be the point of that?

A few more weeks of school go by, and my life settles into a normal rhythm, at least normal enough for me. Martin tutors me once a week, and on weekends Martin, Jez, and I hang out at The Float Boat. Most of the time Everton joins us, too, or we go find him and sit at the table with the candles at the front window of Miles Motors and talk until it's late and Emerson drives everyone home.

When spring break comes, the four of us spend it entirely in each other's company, talking, skating, watching movies. We collect bottles all one day and give almost twenty dollars to the men's shelter. Martin, Everton, and Jez go to see Mr. McGillies in the men's shelter one day, but I find a reason not to go.

And once in a while, Everton and I bundle up and fly to the bottle garden late at night with a flask of hot chocolate, and Celestine and another Spirit Flyer always join us.

Bass Creek has been Rogue-free for a while.

THIRTY-FOUR

Spring comes to Bass Creek all of a sudden. In a flood of gentler weather, the snow starts to melt, and we all discover that last spring's coats and jackets don't fit.

C2 and I walk home one gorgeous spring day, except we don't walk so much as dawdle. For some reason, I feel light and bouncy, like a feather.

We wander into The Float Boat, just because I feel like giving C2 a treat. They're sweet, funny, lovable little kids who haven't beaten anyone up or spat at anyone since the first week of school. They're little individuals who also happen to be twins, and I love them.

They run up to Mrs. Forest and she hands them a candy bag each, and they start picking out jelly beans. As always Christopher grabs the first flavours he comes to, and Christine moves on to the flavour that is next in line in the carefully organized lines of jars. She's stuck with "caramel delight" today, which isn't making her happy. She hates caramel, but she has to take some. That's her rule.

Mrs. Forest helps some kids at a booth and then comes back to the counter.

"Gwendolyn! You see Martin and Everton?"

I shake my head. "Nope."

We look over fondly at the squealing twins, who are buried wrist-deep in jelly bean jars. They're using the candy scoops, though. They do follow the rules better these days, I have to admit.

"Oh! They were in here looking for you earlier. They want me to pass a message along. They have a surprise for you out at the cabin." I sigh. Today is my mother's day to have the phone.

What earthly use is ONE phone per family?

"Okay, thanks, Mrs. Forest. I'll see what they want."

I pay for the candy and we leave. I drag us past Miles Motors, but the shop's closed so I can't ask Emerson if he knows where his little brother is. There's also no way I'll ever call Martin's house, not after his mother phoned the police on me last year, and I don't remember his own number yet.

I'll go out to the cabin with Celestine when Mom gets home and see what they want.

THIRTY-FIVE

I fly above the muddy, frozen spring fields.

Somewhere high above me, Celestine shimmers.

When I called her softly outside my window, she was there in an instant. When I told her I wanted to visit the bottle garden, she agreed.

The Rogue has been silent, little golden sister. My brothers and sisters believe he is in a far distant world. Let us go.

I float over the darkening fallow fields and stop. I'm anchored to the spot where my father found Mr. McGillies. A few barren, leftover stalks rattle in the chilly breeze. I touch down on the muddy road wet from melting snow and walk to the cabin. All dark.

"Everton!" I call. "Martin!" There's no answer.

The cabin's front door bangs in the breeze. It's a lonely sound. I see a new piece of art in the garden. It's a gorgeous bottle tree, bigger than all the bushes. The deepening twilight makes the shapes leap and shrink all around me. I move a little closer to hear the bottles ring. This must be what they wanted to show me.

"Everton! Martin!" I call again. There's no answer, which is weird.

I know he's there before he says anything.

Gwendolyn.

The Rogue stands in the empty cornfield. He's not darkly feathered and gold-eyed; he's just a man with odd green eyes.

I knew you'd come back.

He smiles.

"Where are Martin and Everton?" I have no time to be afraid for myself, but suddenly I feel chilled to the heart for my friends. I'm sure he's done something with them.

I sent them into the woods with Celestine. Never fear, they're fine.

"What did you do with my friends, Abilith?" My voice gets low, and I feel such a sudden hatred for the Rogue that I can barely speak. I will tear him limb from limb if he's hurt them.

They are fine, really. You worry a great deal. But if you must know, I tricked them to look for Celestine, and I tricked her to look for them. So they're all searching the woods together, in a merry goose chase.

"Celestine!" I call loudly. But there is no Celestine shimmering in the sky above me.

"What did you do to her? To Everton and Martin?" I take a step closer to the Rogue, my fists balled in fury.

I have told you before that the Spirit Flyer Celestine is not overly bright, Gwendolyn Golden. She's easily deceived and thinks that your friends are in mortal danger. They are not.

The door of Mr. McGillies's cabin bangs in the wind and I shiver. I stand in muddy spring snow, facing the Rogue all alone. He slowly walks up to me. There's a heat from him, a radiating fire that brushes against my skin. He stops at arm's length, and the sickly sweet smell I remember from the beach reaches me.

It's just us for now.

"Abilith, I will never come with you."

I think you will, Gwendolyn.

"No, I won't."

He stands right next to me. The first shaft of pale moonlight shines on the garden that glints and shimmers like a fairy world. But there are no good fairies here. I stick my chin out.

"My father died right here, being brave. And I'm brave now. I'm not going with you. I'm not Mirandel."

It's all about the way you say things, I'm discovering. There's something in my tone that reaches Abilith, and he stops smiling. He takes a step back, and slowly, like a crane raising mighty wings, he turns into the feathered Rogue. The deep golden eyes blaze at me, and the blackness of his figure and his great wings across his shoulders strike fear in me. He's tall in this form, and he towers above the empty cornfield, glaring down at me.

I try not to cower. I think of the girl in *Misfortunes of the Night Flying Monster, 1447*, and I try to be brave. I look up fearfully.

I grow tired of your games, Gwendolyn Golden. And DO NOT mention Mirandel to me again. You have sent the entire Spirit Flyer community out to catch me, after all I did for you.

"What did you do for me, Abilith?"

I showed you the truth about your father. After that, I would expect some gratitude. But no.

"I'm not afraid of you." What a liar. He stands over me, and I think if I keep talking, Everton and Martin and Celestine will show up any second. I crouch at his feet and look up into the fiery golden eyes.

"You had no right to show me my father's death, Abilith. I didn't ask you to. That was something Mr. McGillies or Mrs. Forest could have told me, when I was older. When I was ready. If it's my story, my truth, what gives you the right to tell me?" A cold wind sweeps across the field, and my teeth chatter. "Celestine and my f-f-friends will s-s-save me," I say, but my voice isn't convincing, not even to me.

Really? I don't see any juvenile humans or incompetent Spirit Flyers around, do you?

The menace wraps around me like a tight arm. But I think *NO!* There's a fire in me somewhere, despite the teeth-chattering cold. My father's feather burns into my chest, and I don't even need to grasp it to get strength from it.

"You're nothing. You're an outcast. I'd never go with you."

I'm incredibly stupid. I've gone too far. The feathered creature narrows his golden eyes.

We'll see about that, Gwendolyn Golden!

With that he raises his hand and a shriek comes from the woods.

Everton and Martin burst from the trees and run toward us, shouting my name.

I have released them. Now let us have some fun.

I leap at him, but Abilith steps away. Martin is suddenly between us. He grabs me and drags me into the cornfield, where we land in the snow and mud.

"Where's Everton!" I gasp, but Abilith sends a shower of sparks into the air, and I can't see a thing. I struggle to stand up but Martin has a vice grip on me. Hot sparks fill the sky and land on the old cabin roof. In a second, there's a lick of flame … and fire.

"Everton!" I scream. I yell again, then I see him.

Everton creeps toward the Rogue. He coils then springs in slow motion, and I know exactly what's going to happen next. Martin holds me tight, but I tear myself free and run across the barren, muddy earth.

The Miles boy? Shall I take him instead of you, Gwendolyn Golden?

"NO!" I shriek. In the corner of my eye I see Celestine land in the cornfield beside Martin, then she is upon Abilith in a twist of white feathers. The two creatures struggle, but Abilith overpowers his sister and pins her with a stream of fire against the cabin. The old building is really on fire now.

Abilith is angry. Furious. He looks for something else to destroy … and his Rogue eye falls upon my friend. I launch myself between Abilith and Everton, but the wicked creature laughs.

Both of you, Gwendolyn Golden? So be it!

Then in a burst of flame and starlight, Everton, the Rogue, and I disappear.

THIRTY-SIX

It's hot.

I'm thirsty.

These two thoughts enter my head at the same time. I *am* hot. And I'm *really* thirsty. I slowly open my eyes.

I don't like what I see at all.

The world is red. Red sand. Red sky. There's a red lake with red water nearby. It's hot, and the water of the red lake bubbles gently. It smells too, like an outhouse. Sulphurous.

My vision clears, and I sense someone nearby.

Everton?

I turn my head, but it seems huge, much too big to be my normal head. Something is very wrong here. I start to panic, but I tell myself to stay calm.

There's someone near me, though. I can hear murmurs. I turn my enormous head a little further to the right, and there he is. Everton. He looks okay. He's wearing his regular black T-shirt and jeans, and he's curled up on the red sand. He's in a cage, a very real cage with thick black bars. It's not a very big cage, though. I doubt he could stand up in it.

Everton, I whisper.

But what comes out of me is not my voice. It's a kind of snort bordering on a roar.

I shake my head in disbelief and try again.

Everton! I say a little louder. There's no mistake this time. I let out a distinctly un-Gwendolyn sound. A roar. A puff of smoke curls up over my nose.

What?

Everton wakes up and rolls over. His eyes focus on me then grow wide with horror. He slides to the back of his cage, and he looks truly terrified. I try to stay perfectly still.

I have no idea what's going on here, but two things are clear enough.

One, Everton is in a cage.

Two, I'm a monster.

I let out a soothing *shhh*, but it sounds like a giant snake hiss, which sends Everton cowering even further to the back of his cage. There's nothing I can do to help him, so I walk away. I might as well try to figure out where we are. But as soon as I take a step, I see my foot move in the sand far below me.

It's very hard not to scream.

My foot is a talon, a leathery, clawed thing a long way down. I take another step, and there's my other talon, huge and heavy and clawed. I gulp, and the smoke rises from my nostrils. I'm getting the picture here.

I'm not just a monster — I'm a dragon.

I twist my enormous head over one shoulder and take a quick peek.

No doubt about it, I'm a dragon, alright. I have spikes down my back, and I'm covered in glittering, deep red scales. I have leathery wings like a small airplane. I even have a long, luxurious tail that disappears off to a tiny point like every description of every dragon that ever was.

I roll one enormous eye toward Everton's cage, and he freezes with terror like a rabbit. I suddenly realize that I'm starving … and Everton might be tasty.

STOP thinking that right NOW!

There's no point in trying to speak, so I say sorry to him in my head, then I drag my enormous belly across the deep red sand. I sound like a chain-link fence scraping across a road. Dragon scales are loud. Who knew?

I clatter across the red beach and dip my scaly head into the red water. I don't care if it's safe. I'm a dragon, and I'm dying of thirst. I drink the red, bubbling, sulphurous ooze.

It's really not that bad.

Abilith has done this to us, and I have to find him. I lean back on my talons, lengthen my throat, and shout with my dragon-voice into the red sky: *ABILITH THE ROGUE! SHOW YOURSELF!*

My mighty bellowing roar echoes across the red lake and through the trees on the other side. A few screeching birds flee from surrounding trees, and an enormous, slithery fish-thing flops into the water from its hiding spot near the beach.

But there's no Rogue Spirit Flyer.

There's no one here but me and a terrified boy in a cage. Wherever we may be.

THIRTY-SEVEN

I lose all sense of time. I almost lose all sense of myself, too.

Whenever I wake up, I'm something else. It makes sense to try to stay awake and remain as just one creature, but it's impossible. Wherever I am, Abilith is in charge of time, space, and reality. He changes my shape at his whim.

I'm a dragon for a while.

Then a huge snake.

Then a horrible crab-like creature that reeks of fish (I'd really like to forget that one). I spend a lot of time in the red, burbling sulphurous stink with just my eyes above the water.

I'm a kind of bird, combined with a lion. A gryphon, I guess.

Once I wake up underwater, so for a while I'm a fish of some sort. Gills are quite an amazing invention.

The next time I wake up, I'm a terrifying, gigantic spider hanging head-down from one of the spindly red trees. Another time I'm a huge girl-sized worm.

I can't lift my head, because technically speaking, I don't have one.

All through these various bodies, only one thing has been the same. Everton. He's locked in his cage, staring at me with terror the entire time, so I try not to go near him. I also try not to think about how delicious he looks. Every single one of the monsters that Abilith turns me into is a meat-eater.

No matter what Abilith does to me, I refuse to gobble up my friend.

In another evil master stroke, Abilith has stricken Everton dumb. He can't speak, so he can't ask the monster he sees before him any questions. There's no way for us to communicate with each other. And somewhere along the way, my father's golden feather disappears, so even that recognizable bit of Gwendolyn is gone.

I try to stay perfectly still until I sleep, but no one can sleep forever. I always wake up.

When I wake up, I do a kind of mental body check and see if my feet feel further or closer to my head than they did when I fell asleep. I check to feel for feet at all, since they may be fins, or scales, or slippery skin. It's a lot like Alice in Wonderland when she eats the mushroom, or is it when she drinks the liquid? In either case, she ends up turning into a monster. Like me.

I spend a lot of time thinking about things like this.

What else am I going to do? Food and water magically appear in Everton's cage, once in the morning and once at night. There's no food for me, though. Just the red water. And Everton. We're thoroughly abandoned. However long we've been here, there's no sign of Abilith. So the most we can do is look at each other from a safe distance. Or sleep.

At first it leaves a person too much time for thinking.

But after a while, it's almost enough to drive someone insane. We have no control over our existence. We have no way of knowing if help and rescue is coming. I think about Celestine and how she said her brothers and sisters were chasing Abilith across the galaxy. I know they will keep looking for him, for us, but if he's not here, how will they find us?

So I try to think about Celestine, to send out thought waves that I'm Gwendolyn, with Everton, and please come and save us.

Like I say, I have no idea how long Everton and I are on Abilith's world. There's no way to know. Seconds, days, months … an eternity.

Then one day I'm a vast, grunting pig with enormous tusks and tiny eyes rooting around for something to eat in the oozy, briny, red muck (pigs can barely see, for the record). A fuzzy shape appears down the beach.

It's Abilith.

I want to run at him. My pig heart goes a little berserk, and there's some wild part of me that wants to tear him through with one of my tusks. I'm also starving, and the thought of his warm blood spilling onto the sand makes me dizzy. I squeal with a terrifying pig rage. Pigs have terrible tempers. Who knew?

I hate him.

I'm just about to rush at him with loathing in my heart, when suddenly ... I'm Gwendolyn again. I'm a girl running along a beach on normal feet, breathing normally. This makes me so giddy for a second that I stop charging toward Abilith and look at my hands. Just normal hands, no feathers, scales, talons, or hooves. For a moment, relief sweeps over me and I slump to the sand, but someone runs up and grabs me. It's Everton. Abilith must have released him from his cage.

Everton clutches me for a second, close to his heart.

"Gwendolyn! You're alive! Those monsters were you?" I nod, but there's no time to chat. Once he realizes I'm me and not an enraged pig, he charges toward our captor who stands with his hands on his hips and smiles. Everton gets close enough to spring, then bounces backward like he hit a wall. Abilith raises his hand at us.

How are my little human guests?

"Let us go," Everton says, getting up. His voice is back, if a little rusty. It's even and steely, and full of loathing.

You sound angry.

"You know the Spirit Flyers will find us and hold a Rogue trial, and you'll be put to death. I would do it now if I could." Everton circles Abilith like a cat about to spring. Abilith looks so calm and cool inside his force field, he's still giving off that too-sweet scent that's just a little stomach-clutching. Too sweet. And false.

"Abilith, let Everton go. You don't even want him, you want me." I say this as calmly as I can, but there's no way to stop the deadly rage in my voice.

"It's a good thing you're behind a force field you coward," Everton hisses. "I'd kill you with my bare hands."

Abilith raises an amused eyebrow.

Now you're just being rude. I come a long way to check on you and you insult me. And threaten me. Perhaps I should teach you some gratitude, Everton Miles?

I can see that the Rogue is going to flatten Everton somehow, and the thought of being alone here forever makes me spring forward until I'm between the two of them. I'd like to say I want to protect Everton from harm, but honestly I'm thinking about myself at the moment.

"Stop. Abilith, leave him alone. Of course we're angry. You've kept us here against our will. You've kept us captive and you haven't told us what you plan to do with us. You've turned me into monsters, and I'm starving. What do you want from us? The Spirit Flyers have rescued me once before, what makes you think they won't do it again?"

I've had a lot of time to think about what I'd say to Abilith if and when he showed up. My main plan has always been to remain calm, as calm as possible, and not to show fear. And also to keep him talking until I can think of something, some way out of this prison.

You're not very bright, are you, Gwendolyn? I expected more from you. Do you think I would keep you in the same place? This is a new bubble world of my own creation. They will never find you here, and as you have no doubt noticed, I keep changing your shape. And Everton cannot be detected inside the cage, so even if the Spirits come close, they will not see two children. They will see only you, a monster.

A fact. Why did he tell me that? Did I detect fear? What is Abilith doing here if not checking that we're still safe? I've had a lot of time on my hands lately to think things through. My thought processes seem faster and sharper than I remember them before. Being alone with your thoughts maybe isn't all that bad.

"You're lying. Because that's what you are, Abilith. A liar, a deviant, and an outcast. You know that the Spirit Flyers are closing in, and that's why you're here. To check on us."

A flicker of fear crosses his face, but Abilith recovers quickly. He raises his arms and turns back into his feathered self, casting a giant shadow across the red beach, malevolence and heat hitting Everton and me like a fierce wind. The red sand starts to blow in our faces, the red water starts to bubble and burn. The red sky turns darker, darker, then almost black, while blood-red clouds form a thunderous booming.

YOU. DO. NOT. CALL. ME. A. LIAR. GWEN-DOLYN. GOLDEN.

"But that's what you are. A sad, lonely, frightened, powerless, and friendless … *liar.*"

As I say these words, I edge closer to Everton. I eye the beach. Where can we run? There's no cover. Abilith grows in height until we have to strain our necks to see his face. His golden eyes look like fire from the beach, and he looms over us, the storm around us raging higher and higher.

Everton tries to protect me. He puts his arms around me, but the sand whips so hard against us that there's no protection anywhere. I try not to shriek as we huddle together beneath the enormous and rage-filled demon above us.

THAT, GWENDOLYN GOLDEN, WAS A MISTAKE.

Then Abilith the Rogue splits the world apart, and Everton and I are falling, falling, falling through the blackest clouds, through a storm that never ends. My second-last thought is about demons and pitchforks, and the *Monster Meets Her End, 1449.*

My last thought, though, is that unlike the girl in T. Bosch's drawing, I'm not falling into oblivion alone.

THIRTY-EIGHT

You can fall for an eternity.

After a while you stop hearing the wind in your ears, or the scream of the person you are falling with. Your heartbeat stops rushing, and you become almost peaceful. There's no talking in the falling world either. It's not all that pleasant. Your voice gets shoved back into your throat, so you fall silently, like feathers, like ash.

Falling isn't all that different from floating.

Everton and I fall and fall. We lock hands a few times, but it's too hard to fall like that, so we have to let go. I sleep, I pass through hunger and thirst and anything remotely human and binding me to the world. I have time to think, slow and long thoughts. I think about Martin collecting bottles for Mr. McGillies. I think about high school, and how sad it is that I won't be able to finish it. I think about C2 and Dr. Adam Parks, and Huckleberry Finn and Jim. At least those two had an *ending*, I think with envy. Even Alice got to the bottom of the rabbit hole. Maybe my ending will just be to fall forever and ever, which isn't an ending at all.

I think about my old dog Cassie and how worried my mother must be. My poor mother. Now two of her loved ones have gone missing because of Night Flying.

We fall, we float, the wind rushes in our ears, for a long time. We fall for so long that I really have no sense of my body anymore, where it starts, where it ends, what it needs, what pains or delights it.

Then … I hear a buzzing in my right ear.

For a while, I ignore the buzz. But the buzz is insistent. Then it gets louder. I've heard this buzzing before. I already know what it is. I'm dulled from falling, but I can still panic. There out of the darkness an enormous black cloud hurtles toward us.

The Shade.

It roars like a giant black sky monster with all the sadness of the world rolled up into it. The roar gets louder, a tidal wave of pity and despair, the landing place for the lost and unloved of the world.

The Shade is coming for Everton and me. We flee, or we die.

"FLY, EVERTON!"

"WHAT?"

"FLY! FLY! THE SHADE!"

Everton looks behind me, and his eyes widen with fear. The last time I met the Shade, I had no idea what it was, and I was new to flying. Not this time. Everton and I scream through space. We're rockets, we're comets, we're stardust. We're not falling anymore. Now we're shrieking through the emptiness, fleeing for our lives. There's a blackness, a void of despair filled with a thousand, thousand crying voices hot on our heels, but I have more strength now, more skill, and more importantly, I have Everton. We fly so fast that starshine zips past us, and I hear the voices in the Shade calling us: YOU CANNOT FLY, GWENDOLYN GOLDEN!

So I just fly faster.

Everton and I are streaks of starlight. Where are we going? How long do we flee? We shriek past planets, past asteroids, past whatever that was, a cosmic fury, perhaps … and the Shade is right there, just off our toes, calling and whining and weeping at us to give up and die in its arms.

We fly for ages, but we can't do this forever. We're tiring, we fly, we fly, we fly … then I hear a shriek. I turn and the last thing I see is Everton's terrified face as he disappears into the darkness chasing us.

"DON'T SAVE ME! SAVE YOURSELF, GWENDOLYN!" His final words echo in my ears.

What choice do I have? I don't even hesitate, because what would be the point? All my life has led up to this moment.

I turn and fly headfirst into the Shade.

THIRTY-NINE

The stars are gone. The void is blackness and fear. And it's cold. There is nothing. No sound. No movement. No colour. I'm surrounded by a solid black nothingness.

I'm utterly alone. Which is surprising, because the Shade is made of lost souls that a few seconds ago were screaming my name. Now that I'm one of them, they don't seem to care for me.

"Everton?" I say, but the Shade is a noise-eater. My words barely leave my lips before they are silenced.

"EVERTON!" I scream, but my voice is muffled and dies. There's no screaming in the Shade.

Maybe I'm dead, so I have no voice? I really don't feel dead, though, that's the thing. I lift my hand to my throat and there's definitely a pulse. If I were dead, would I think to take my pulse? Would I have one?

I walk a little, but it's impossible to tell if I'm moving since there's nothing to walk upon. I whisper "Everton!" a few more times, but my voice goes nowhere.

There is only more nothing.

I have two choices. Give up. Or fight.

I'm not about to give up. I have to find Everton and get us out of here.

What is the opposite of dead, I wonder? Very, very alive somehow. Who are the most alive people I can imagine?

My little brother and sister pop into my head. Suddenly, I'm flooded with thoughts of C2. Being born, being little babies that my mom and I carry around in their car seats, one each. They're toddlers that we chase through the park, then school-age kids that I hold by the hand and take to class. I think so deeply about my very alive brother and sister that it takes me a moment to notice the small change in the air around me.

There's a tiny lightening, a greyness in the black. I think harder about C2. I see Christopher wind up and toss a newspaper in a perfect arc onto a neighbour's front porch. I see Christine's angry little face, and I hear her shriek, "STINKY!"

And something moves past me. With a gentle whoosh, a breath of wind blows past my arm.

Something's happening. So I think harder about my life. About creating a goblet that doesn't leak, and how Chas believed I could do it from the start. I think about Martin helping Mr. McGillies and the lovely bottle garden he and Everton created. I think about Jez walking me to Adam's office. I think about Adam handing me the tissue box.

"I want to live." It just pops out of me, and I've never known something to be more true.

More wind moves past me, and the darkness is lighter, greyer. There's movement and I hear shuffling, murmurs.

Then I see them.

A thousand, thousand souls, dead, definitely dead, shuffle toward me, drawn to me, the live thing in their midst. Dead moths to my living flame. Figures shuffle all around me. A face comes close and I draw in my breath. An old man with limp hair and fallen eyes, or what would have been a man if he were alive, shuffles past on silent feet. He murmurs something I can't make out. Then more faces pass by, all murmuring softly. Old women, old men, the middle-aged, the young. The children are the hardest. I simply cannot look at the pale, empty faces of the little children as they shuffle by.

The dead move past, unseeing.

I take a deep breath.

If thinking about being alive draws the dead to me, maybe I can draw Everton to me as well? So I close my eyes and think harder about us. I think about a pair of dark blue eyes and a boy in workboots and a winter coat knocking at my window. I think about Celestine and her older brother guarding Everton and me in the moonlight winter garden of glass just so we can enjoy its beauty. I think about a boy in a cage who refuses to give in to fear.

The darkness around me gets lighter, and the wave of trudging souls speeds up. I pay attention to my feet and begin to shuffle into the darkness, sweeping my arms in front of me. The dead veer away like a cloud in a gust of wind. Like a volleyball with me at the net.

"Everton! Everton!" I whisper again and again, but there's no answer. The cold makes my fingers and toes tingle. I shuffle forward, a spark of life pushing upstream against a river of death. I'm not giving up. I sweep my arms and whisper for my friend.

Then there's a movement ahead of me, a real sound, not just dead air and shuffling. Someone is crying. I move faster, like pushing through thigh-deep water. But the darkness is lighter somehow, and then I bang into something solid. A real body.

Everton.

He turns and sees me. He looks so heartbroken that I can only clasp him to me.

"Don't cry, Everton," I whisper.

He stares at two figures shuffling toward us. A man and woman with dead eyes. They murmur something that I can't make out.

"I can hear them," Everton cries softly.

"Who?"

"My mother, my father." The grey man and woman stop and turn toward us. Their grey hair, their empty eyes, their murmurs mean nothing to me. They look like all the other lost souls in this foul place.

"How do you know it's them?" I whisper.

"They're calling me!" He covers his face with his hands, and I hug him with all my strength.

"Everton, no! It's not them. Not what they were, not the good parts. Just a sad memory. The handbook told me. You have to get up! Get up,

Everton!" But it's no use. He's on his knees, his face hidden in his hands. My heart just about breaks, and all I can do is gently stroke his hair.

We are lost. We are forsaken. We are going to die.

"Celestine! Celestine, please help us!" I whisper. I think it with all my heart. I reach out with whatever is left of me and I think, *Celestine, help us! We're dying! We're in the Shade! It's your little golden sister! It's Gwendolyn!*

Then I hear him.

My father walks slowly toward me on dead feet. His head is low, his eyes downcast, but there is no doubt that he is speaking in the strange, rustling, whisper-voice of the place. This time though, I hear him perfectly.

Gwendolyngwendolyngwendolyngoldengolden-goldenmylovemylovemylove

I gasp. If ever I was going to break, it's now.

But there is something in me that won't break. I could have broken lots of times before now, in Everton's car, in Adam's office, on Abilith's world. But I didn't. And suddenly it's clear to me: I'm not going to.

My father's gentle voice hangs in the air. He turns briefly toward me and hesitates, then shuffles past. As he moves by, I can't help it. I reach out and try to touch him, but he's only air, darkness, a shifting wisp. Then he's gone.

"Goodbye. I love you too," I whisper.

My father vanishes with the crowd. I hold on to Everton. We must look so broken. Who will help us?

Celestine! Save us! We need you!

As soon as I say her name this time, the sky in the distance opens just for a second and I see stars. I wrench Everton to his feet and clasp him with all my strength, which isn't easy. He's a lot bigger than me.

"Everton, call Celestine!" My voice cracks. More dead people shuffle by, whispering and downcast. A child, two children, a teenager, a young woman, an old man, all wandering and whispering, lost, lost, lost in the darkness. Everton moans but looks at me.

I shout, which comes out as a weird low murmur. "Everton! I was thinking of Celestine and I just saw stars! There's light! There's an end to the Shade!"

Everton shakes his head but says, "Celestine? Stars?"

"Yes!"

He blinks but concentrates. The darkness is greyer still, and the thousands of dead seem further away. He wraps his arms around me, and I lay my head on his chest as we both whisper Celestine's name, over and over.

We are gentle, we are brave, and we have each other. Whatever happens to us, whether we survive or not, Everton holds me close and I hold him.

Little golden sister! Do not despair!

Celestine! Over Everton's shoulder, a tiny light glimmers in the distance and I see stars again, and my heart leaps up. I bury my face in his chest.

"Help us Celestine, come fast!"

The sky really is lighter. For an instant the Shade closes in tightly all around us, then Celestine arrives with a brilliance that's actually not all that easy to bear. After all the darkness we've been through, I cry out and shield my face. But Celestine sweeps into the heart of the Shade and gathers Everton in one arm and me in the other. I have a weird thought: what a great T. Bosch drawing this would make. He'd call it *The Night Flyers' Rescue*.

Definitely one for the *Night Flyer's Handbook*.

More blinding Spirit Flyers surround us as we speed away from the Shade.

I turn under the great white wing in time to see the Shade vanish. Stars appear behind the darkness, and the Shade is gone. A shout from a thousand, thousand voices fills the air. I hear one shout, one beloved laugh, louder than all the others.

My father, like all the other souls trapped in the Shade, is free.

This fills me with such incredible joy that for a moment I struggle to be let go, but Celestine has me in a vice grip, and we shriek away through the stars. I have to content myself with a silent goodbye. My hand moves to grasp my father's golden feather, but then I remember it's gone. Except it's not. It'll always be next to my heart.

Then we slow, there are trees. A clearing. At the last moment we gently touch down in the middle of a forest of tall trees. We land on solid ground. Our fall is over. We've defeated the Shade for now, and all it took was a family of starshot immortals, the memory of my father ...

... and Everton Miles, my strange and beautiful friend.

FORTY

We stand in the centre of a ring of trees in an ancient forest. I've seen these trees before. It's the clearing we used last summer at the Midsummer Party.

I'm dizzy, disoriented, and lean against Everton, who wraps one arm around me. Mrs. Forest and Emerson run into the clearing, calling our names. I dive into Mrs. Forest's arms, and Everton does the same with his brother.

We're safe, we're really here, among our friends. As soon as I can breathe, questions boil out of me.

"Mrs. Forest, what happened to us? What year is this?"

She holds me tight and says, "You're at the sacred forest ring. This is the only safe place you could land. No time has passed, or barely any. It's still the day you vanished. You're free of the Rogue."

Everton and I look at each other, and I'm not ashamed to say that we're both full of tears. I hug him again, and he takes my face in his hands and then gently, ever so gently, he kisses me on the forehead.

"I cannot tell you how happy I was to see that pig turn into you," he whispers.

No one else seems to notice, or they pretend not to. Mrs. Forest, Emerson, and even Celestine seem suddenly very interested in the treetops.

They come.

Celestine's sweet voice makes us all look up. Above us, drifting from the heavens like maple keys spinning from the trees, are dozens of Spirit Flyers. They're so brilliant that it's hard to look at them. They slowly descend into our midst through the treetops.

A darkness is at their centre.

Abilith.

His hands are bound and his wings are tied tightly to his body, but he looks defiant.

The Spirit Flyers land in the forest clearing with their captive.

One of the Spirit Flyers, perhaps the oldest of the group (but it's almost impossible to tell one from the other so I can't be sure), speaks in my head.

Gwendolyn Golden, please step forth.

I walk over. I'm still unsteady on my feet. Everton comes with me and holds me up. I try to focus on the Spirit Flyer and what he's saying.

This Rogue has abducted you twice and held you captive. He has tormented you and your friend, Everton Miles. He has told you truths that you would have discovered on your own, in your own time, when you were ready.

"Yes," I say. "All that's true." The tone of the Spirit Flyer is solemn, and I start to worry. What exactly is going on here?

It is our belief that he will not stop pursuing you, for he is incapable of temperance and moderation. He is outcast among us for an ancient misdeed. We do not easily kill one another, but if you wish it, we will destroy him.

Destroy him? I can barely concentrate on what the Spirit Flyer is saying to me. All I want is to go home. I force myself to look into Abilith's fiery eyes. He skulks between the Spirit Flyers at his sides. This creature has just turned me into a monster. Monsters. I've lived in fear of him all winter. I don't want to be afraid anymore. Whether I'm up to this or not, I have to face him.

I clear my throat.

"Is this a Rogue trial?"

The Spirit Flyer inclines his head, which I take to mean "yes."

Mrs. Forest says, "They're tired. Can't they rest?" But the Spirit Flyer shakes his head this time.

We must decide now. You know his nature, Emmeline Forest. He is devious, and if we wait he will only escape us. What is his fate, Gwendolyn Golden?

I look at Abilith, who drops his gaze. I look at Celestine, Mrs. Forest, and then my eyes stop on Everton. I take a deep breath.

"I don't want to decide his fate. I'm too young to carry the weight of his death on my conscience all my life. You're his brothers and sisters. You cast him out. You have to decide what to do with him. He's your responsibility."

I look at the Spirit Flyer.

"I can't speak for Everton, but I don't want to be the one who decides if the Rogue lives or dies."

"Neither do I," Everton says at my side.

All the Spirit Flyers look at me, which is a bit unnerving. I try not to fidget. Abilith hangs his head low, and he looks small between the enormous Spirit Flyers on either side of him.

"You have him now. Can't you just keep him chained? Or imprisoned somehow?" I ask. As soon as I say it, I realize it would never work. Abilith, all the Spirit Flyers, are creatures of the air, of light or darkness in his case, and they roam the galaxies. How do you imprison a creature like that?

If this is to be my trial, let me speak.

It's Abilith. He raises his head to look at me. Everton slips his hand into mine. The head Spirit Flyer seems angry but answers.

You may speak, Rogue, but do not bore us with lies.

So Abilith begins, looking only at me. I refuse to look away.

You have cast me out and condemned me to an eternity of lonely wandering. If you kill me, so be it. I will be done with this existence. But before you kill me, hear me.

Gwendolyn, here is the truth about my crime: long ago, when your kind was building great cathedrals of stone and exploring the watery globe in tiny wooden ships, I loved a human woman. We had a child, a perfect child, a girl.

The head Spirit Flyer says in a cool, golden, smooth voice, *Do not make yourself sound so noble,*

*Rogue. What you did is to break the one law — the
ONE LAW — of our kind.*

Abilith seems to not hear and continues, still
looking at me.

*That child was the lovely Mirandel. You cannot
imagine my delight at watching my child grow, for our
kind does not have young. Mirandel was perfect. From
her mother she had green eyes and dark, wavy hair, and
in every way reminds me of you, Gwendolyn Golden.
This is why I sought you out, for you are an exact match
for my Mirandel. You could have been twins.*

This shocks me. I see the girl being pushed along
by pitchforks or falling in T. Bosch's art and realize
it must be Mirandel, which also explains why the girl
in the drawing looks so much like me.

*From me, her father, Mirandel received the gift of
flight, and so she was a Night Flyer. Her mother hid her
among the humans of her village and instructed her
not to fly, but the Spirit Flyers discovered her one night,
floating over the village cornfield. They soon realized
that I was her father.*

*For this, my brothers and sisters have cast me out,
although I was not the first Rogue to love a human.
There have been many children, many Night Flyers,
many Rogue Spirit Flyers, although I am the last.
Gwendolyn Golden, your kind are all sprung from
one like me.*

Abilith says all this with the saddest look. So I'm
the product of a long-ago love between a Rogue
Spirit Flyer and a human? Not a terribly appealing
thought, frankly. Everton, Emerson, Mrs. Forest,

my father, all of us Night Flyers all over the planet are one part Rogue.

The Spirit Flyers draw together and murmur. I think being reminded of past Rogues has them upset. The leader speaks again, and he sounds mad.

You are not the only Rogue, Abilith, that is true, but we will see to it that you are the last. Since the selfish actions of the first Rogue, since the first Night Flyer children appeared on the planet, we have befriended them and cared for them. But your offspring are persecuted and condemned. They must live in fear and hiding. It is only now that Night Flyers are not burned and tortured as witches. Have you ever seen a Night Flyer burned at the stake as a witch, Abilith? I think not. You and the other Rogues are too cowardly to see the final result of what you have done. Thankfully, few people believe in witches on this planet anymore.

Abilith looks unbowed. *I saved Mirandel from the fire. I saw her suffering at the hands of villagers who did not understand what she was. I was determined to save my child. So I left her gifts. I became her friend. Then I asked if she wanted to be with me, her father. I could show her how to fly and the wonders of the world that I inhabit. She came with me.*

The Spirit Flyers don't seem to believe him.

You stole a human child, Rogue. She was not yours to take.

Abilith holds his head up higher. His next words are just for me.

Mirandel came willingly, and she loved me, her father. I saved her from a fiery death at the hands of cruel men who feared her. That's the truth, although I know you don't want to believe it.

Something has been decided, since the Spirit Flyers make a tight circle around Abilith, and the lead Spirit Flyer turns to all of us.

It is a very pretty story, Gwendolyn Golden, but it is a lie. No doubt given the choice between being burned alive or held captive with Abilith, Mirandel chose life. The Rogue is incapable of telling the truth. Think about how he treated you and Everton, then consider how he treated Mirandel. Was she free? Was she happy? Ask yourself this: would your father, or any loving father, keep a child against their will?

I shake my head.

We accept that you do not want to decide his fate, and so we now remove the Rogue forever, where he can no longer cause pain to you or your kind.

"Please, don't make him suffer," I say to my astonishment.

The Spirit Flyer tilts his head and answers me gently. *You are merciful, Gwendolyn Golden. That is a great strength, and one of the many reasons why we cherish your kind. Whatever our decision, your plea will be considered. We may find a tiny, uninhabited galaxy and lock him there, our prisoner for eternity.*

With those final words, the Spirit Flyers leave with Abilith in a blaze of light, and he looks at me as he disappears. This time there is no doubt: tears are in those strange golden eyes, but are they tears of sadness or regret? Or is he only sorry for himself and his lost freedom?

I will never know. I do know this: no father, not Huck's, not Shelley Norman's, not even a Rogue father from long ago, can hurt us and say it is for love.

As the Spirit Flyers drift upward with their prisoner, a single black feather falls into my open hand, burns to ash, and blows away with the gentle breeze.

FORTY-ONE

Emerson drives us home. Being in a car, having my own form back, knowing Abilith is gone forever ... it's almost too much to take in.

When Everton and I arrive at my house, my mother says hello and tells me dinner is in ten minutes. I hug my mother, brother, and sister, who all seem a little surprised. No one suspects a thing has happened to us or that in our heads we've been away for ages. The only one of my family members who seems a little put out is Cassie. Maybe I still smell like dragon?

No one even missed us.

Except for poor Martin. I have to admit, I completely forgot about him.

Everton and I are eating a plate of cheese and crackers on my bed, since we're starving. Although we were only gone a short time from this world, the memory of starvation lingers. I'm not being terribly ladylike. I have the box of crackers clutched to my chest when the front doorbell rings. My mother talks to someone, then we hear feet on the stairs and Martin sticks his head in my bedroom.

He looks stricken.

"What happened to you?" he asks quietly.

"Oh, Martin, we're so sorry! You must have been worried. Cracker?" I offer him the box, which is very, very mature of me, but he crosses his arms.

"You both vanished! That Abilith creature burned Mr. McGillies's cabin to the ground. The other one, Celestine I think you called her, she took off after you. I was all alone. I called the fire department, but by the time they arrived there was nothing left."

"How's the glass garden?" Everton asks. We both feel remorseful. Martin is covered in mud, and his pants are soaking wet. We've had time to dry out on Abilith's baking world. We're toasty and warm. Martin looks like he has suffered almost as much as us.

"It's fine. At least it was when I left. I RAN into town because no one was answering the phone at The Float Boat. I didn't know where else to go. Luckily, Mr. Forest was just getting off the phone when I got there and told me you were both fine. So I came here." Martin is sad and worried and put out at both of us.

"Martin, we've been through more than you can imagine," Everton says quietly. "But close the door, and we'll tell you everything."

Which we do. It takes a while. My mother brings us each a tray of dinner (chicken, mashed potatoes, and peas have never been so delicious), which we eat at the desk in my bedroom while we talk. Martin listens intently and finally says, "I'm glad you're okay." Frankly, it's possible that he doesn't believe us and thinks this is a weird hoax.

Poor Martin.

Whether he believes us or not, the three of us are now closer than ever. Everton and I return to school, and we're inseparable. Martin and Jez hang out with us at lunch and between classes, and on the weekends the four of us spend most of our time together, either studying at the library or visiting Mr. McGillies's bottle garden. Between the three of us, Martin, Everton, and I fill Jez in on everything that happened, and it's so, so nice not to be the only one to bear the burden of the truth.

Or the telling.

For the rest of the school year, every Saturday Martin and I collect bottles along the main street and donate the money to the men's homeless shelter. We've donated about $75 now. It's good to spend time with Martin, he's so normal.

He tutors me right until the end of school, and I pass everything with a respectable B average. I even create a six-piece set of leak-free goblets in pottery class, which makes Chas ecstatic. I give them to my mother as an end-of-school gift from her eldest, and she seems to like them. I think she might even use them.

Apart from the abduction by an ancient fallen Spirit and a journey among the terrified dead of the Shade, grade nine really wasn't that hard.

We all slip into summer and this year, I get a job. I hang out at Miles Motors so much with Everton that his brother ends up hiring us both. I wear a huge oil-covered jumpsuit (which I adore), and I learn how to change a flat tire, how to start a dead car battery, and how to top up the windshield wiper fluids. It's fun and practical. Mom brings her car by a lot for some reason and sits and has coffee with Emerson while Everton and I top up her already full windshield wiper fluid bottle.

They seem to have a lot to say to each other. I hear a lot of laughter between them at the table in the front window of the store, and when I ask Everton about it he smiles and whispers, "Emerson isn't that much younger than your mom." Which is cryptic, until I get it and then think *ohhhh*! Then … *Well, that might be okay actually*.

As soon as school is over, Everton and I fly. Every night. We just fly. Sometimes Jez and Martin follow below on their bicycles, sometimes not. But soon they can't keep up, since we go further and further from our little town, and one night Everton and I get halfway to the city before we stop. We sit on a huge hill looking toward the bright lights that seem so close.

"One day soon I'm going to live there," I say. Everton is chewing a huge wad of gum. He smiles.

"I want to travel. There are Night Flying communities all over the world. What about flying in … Hawaii?" He snuggles a little closer and stops short of putting his arm around me. We'll always be close.

No matter what happens, as the only two teenage Night Flyers in town, we'll be spending plenty of time together. A lifetime, probably.

The sky is pink in the east before I get home, tired but rejuvenated.

Soon it'll be time for the Midsummer Party.

But before that happens, there's one more important thing I have to do.

FORTY-TWO

I'm in the hospital waiting room perched on a hard plastic chair. It's boiling outside, a hot summer day, and the air conditioning fan blasts cold air onto my head.

"Come on, Gwen," Martin says. "His room is right there." Martin has no idea why I'm stuck in the chair. I can't move. "He wants to see you."

After we collected bottles today, Martin dragged me here to see Mr. McGillies, and I couldn't think of a lie fast enough to say no. He's been back and forth between the shelter and the hospital for a while. I've lost track of how many times.

THINK, GWENDOLYN! What on earth are you going to say to the man who killed your father?

No, my reasonable voice says. *He didn't kill your father. The Shade did that.*

Martin touches my arm.

"Are you okay?" he asks gently.

"I really don't like hospitals. You go in first. I'll go in after you."

Every single part of me doesn't want to be here. Suddenly all I can think of is springing out of the chair and lighting out for the territories. But I'm not Huckleberry Finn. People know me, understand me — even care for me.

What would my father want me to do? What could I possibly do to make him proud of me?

I stood up to Abilith the Rogue. I was all manner of monster, I survived the Shade, and I stood judge over a Rogue trial. What's so scary about a little old man?

Other people walk by the hospital room. Nurses, orderlies, doctors, quiet families. Everyone else is here for quite sad reasons, too. I'm not the only one. I bite my nails and squirm around on the terrible chair in the freezing air. Martin comes out of Mr. McGillies's room. "He's awake. I told him you were here to see him."

I take a deep breath and stand up. "I'll come with you, Gwen." Martin says. But I shake my head.

Then I go into Mr. McGillies's hospital room alone.

Life is never what you expect.

Mr. McGillies is so tiny in the enormous hospital bed. As soon as the door shushes closed behind me, I walk over and take his tiny brown hand. I don't even hesitate, although I was expecting to stand by the door and stare.

Funny, that's not what happens.

I hold his small, warm hand and look down at his shrunken face. He's all yellow. He was never yellow.

Machines are all around him beeping and shushing quietly, and there's a gentle thump-thumping that sounds like a little bird heartbeat. I guess it's his.

His eyes are closed. Just like him to make me speak first. I clear my throat.

"Mr. McGillies. It's me, Gwendolyn Golden." He doesn't move or seem to hear me, but he never shows much emotion when I talk to him on the street. Why would now be any different? Although this being my first sickbed moment, I can't say how people would behave.

Drip.

"I know my dad died saving you, Mr. McGillies." It just tumbles out. Wow. It wasn't even all that hard.

Drip.

"My mom deserved a husband. I deserved a dad. My little brother and sister did too," I say. At the mention of C2, my voice trembles. But this time the faucet doesn't burst. Sure the faucet drips, but just a little.

"But it's not your fault. It was never your fault. I'm proud that my dad tried to save you. I want you to know that I know the truth, that's all."

There's no reaction from him that I can see, which is making me a bit uncomfortable. I wait a few moments, but there's no answer, although it's possible that the gentle thump-thump of his heart-beat goes a tiny bit faster. I try to think of something else to say.

"Um, Martin is still collecting bottles for you every Saturday and donating the money to the men's shelter. He probably told you that. I help him sometimes. And, um … I hear that you taught art to kids and were a chess champion. Maybe when you get out of here, you can teach me chess? Your bottle garden is really nice. We go there a lot. I hope you can see it soon. It's pretty when the moonlight shines on it in the winter, but it's nice in the summer moonlight, too."

I watch his yellowed face a moment longer, but there's still no answer.

"Goodbye, Mr. McGillies." As I turn to leave, his brown eyes pop open.

"Gwendolyn." It's hard for him to talk. His voice sounds as hot and dry as sand, so I lean in a little.

"Yes, Mr. McGillies?"

"Why were you watching me all summer?"

I'm surprised he knows this. "Maybe I was looking out for you, Mr. McGillies," I say, and it's partly true.

"Like your dad," he says. I gulp and nod.

He lies still and keeps his eyes closed, then he draws a deep breath.

"I was his Watcher, too."

"Oh!" I've never thought about this before. I guess my dad would have had a Watcher, like me. I'm suddenly warmed by the thought of Mr. McGillies pushing his bottle cart around town watching after my Night Flyer dad when he was young, then doing the same thing for me years later. Mr. McGillies could probably tell me a lot of stories about my dad.

"Your dad took better care of me than I did of him, though." Mr. McGillies sounds a little sad.

"No, that's not true! You saved his daughter. You saved me from the Shade last year, Mr. McGillies. I think my dad would thank you for that, don't you?"

He finally looks at me with those big, brown eyes, and then he smiles. Same old smile.

"Missy … needs a new Watcher," he says, then falls back exhausted. He can't speak anymore, he's too tired.

"I don't want a new Watcher," I say.

Drip. Drip. I really have to get out of here.

"Goodbye, get better soon." And I walk out of there as fast as I can.

Tears blur my vision, but there's nothing wrong with my hearing. As I walk through the door a tiny, birdlike voice croaks, "Don't fly away now, missy!"

FORTY-THREE

A few days later, it's midsummer, and I turn fifteen.

We have a surprisingly large birthday party out at Mr. McGillies's bottle garden, which has now become a proper picnic spot for the town. Since the old cabin burned down, Bass Creek has taken an interest in the place and bought an acre of field from the farmer. It turns out that Mr. McGillies never actually owned the land he built his cabin on, but the farmer didn't have the heart to evict him.

Now as well as the bottle garden, there are regular picnic tables, flowers in planters, and permanent barbecues, and families go to have picnic dinners and catch a breeze over the field. The farmer put up a hay bale maze for the kids, and the town is talking about building a wading pool. We need more fun in this town, so I applaud it. There are bottle donation bins, and every week they're emptied and the money goes to the local men's shelter.

My mom, C2, and I go out early and decorate the cornfield with a banner that says "Happy 15th

GG," and I get the barbecue going with a little help from Everton, who has shown up early. Mr. and Mrs. Forest arrive carrying a huge white cake with a marzipan angel just like last year, and Jez and Martin struggle out of the back of their car with plates and cups and party napkins.

Miss Moreau and Mr. Tupperman show up together, and they bring a badminton set and everyone takes turns losing the birdies in the cornfield. The nice people who run the men's shelter come too, since I've gotten to know them pretty well from dropping off a donation every Saturday. I invited Jeffrey Parks when I saw him on the street a few days earlier, and he shows up with his uncle Adam, who outside his office is just a big, goofy happy guy, and they stay long enough to sing "Happy Birthday" and have some cake, then they're going camping for the rest of the summer.

We barbecue hot dogs, play badminton, walk the hay bale maze, and I sit alone for a while by the arch and watch my friends having fun, Night Flyers and non-Night-Flyers together, and I know this is my community, all of them.

Mr. McGillies isn't getting better, but he's not worse either and one day soon Martin, Everton, and I are going to bring him here in Everton's car and let him sit in his wheelchair and look at what all those years of collecting bottles actually accomplished. I look out at the trees, and although I can't be sure, there may be a rustle of white feathers for a moment, and a gentle whisper of *Gwendolyn* in a voice I don't mind at all.

Abilith is gone.

So is my dad, but I'll always love him, and it's okay to think about him whenever I want. So I do. And it's mostly just happy little kid memories. At least I haven't tripped over a sad one yet. I even start sharing some of my memories of him with my little brother and sister. They can't get enough.

I watch my friends and family eat cake and play badminton. Everton and Martin are trying to teach Mrs. Forest how to play, and I can't help but smile. The late afternoon sun shines on us, the new corn is growing high, and the bottles ring in the garden.

The big surprise for my birthday is my OWN phone. Jez helps me set it up, and the first text I get is from Everton, who is standing alone in the bottle archway.

It says, *You were a beautiful dragon.*

FORTY-FOUR

After my birthday party, it's time for the Night Flyer Midsummer party.

It's 12:03, and I wait by my open bedroom window. I'm fiddling with my own golden feather, the one from my box-book under the bed, the one all Night Flyers take to the party.

I'm dressed all in white, just like last year. Everton shows up a few minutes later, and we drift gently out of town. It's a gorgeous night, and I have to say that Everton looks quite nice in a white tuxedo (bit of overkill though, maybe). This year I have no trouble flying all the way to the forest where the Spirit Flyers will meet us, and as I drift along I think how different my first trip to the Midsummer party was. On this night last year, I had to keep stopping to rest and float on my back, and Mrs. Forest let me play in the corn when I needed a break.

I don't need a break this year. Instead, we just float and soon enough we get to the huge, ancient trees and slowly float into the forest.

When we arrive at the clearing where I stood judge at a Rogue Trial not so long ago, all the Night Flyers from last year's party are gathered: ancient Gramelda Insted, Chan, Rajiv, Dean and Drew Evershot and their daughter Diana, Sofie and Sarah, Mrs. Forest, Emerson, Everton, and me.

Except this year there are a few additions I wasn't expecting.

Once Everton and I touch down and say hello to everyone, two Spirit Flyers lead five people gently into the ring. They're blindfolded.

My mother removes her blindfold first, and then Christine and Christopher remove theirs. They come and give me a hug. Earlier tonight my mother and I told C2 the truth about me. They took it surprisingly well. They didn't even ask any questions. I'm glad they finally know I'm a Night Flyer. It's been hard to hide it, and I'm all about the truth these days. Jez and Martin take their blindfolds off too and look a little bewildered and shy. I guess I can see why. Spirit Flyers are tall and winged and brilliant white, and well … they're spirits.

When we're all arranged in a circle, the head Spirit Flyer begins.

Tonight is a very special time for us. We rejoice, we celebrate, and we also welcome Gwendolyn Golden, who has had one year to choose if she will become a Night Flyer for life, or if she will choose to be earthbound forever. There are wise reasons to choose either path.

The Spirit Flyer turns to Martin, Jez, and my family.

As Gwendolyn's best friends and her family members, you have been invited to this sacred event, and we welcome you. First, we must allow Gwendolyn Golden to give us her answer. Please step forth.

I step into the middle of the circle, my heart pounding. I have tried very, very hard not to think about this moment. I know my mother would be happy if I decided to give up Night Flying. It scares her, and it should. She has already lost one loved one to the Shade, and it's not an easy life. You're always on the brink of being discovered. Not so long ago, I would have been burned at the stake. Plus, there are real dangers out there waiting for you.

I look over at my family, and my mom looks like she'd like to cry, but my brother and sister are both grinning at me. Jez and Martin, my non-flying friends, both look a little overwhelmed, to be honest. I look at Mrs. Forest , who is as happily married as anyone I ever met, and Mr. Forest isn't a Night Flyer. Then I look at the rest of the people in the ring and stop at Everton.

Gwendolyn Golden, you must give us your decision.

The warm evening brushes past my cheek, and I look up at the stars.

I take a deep breath and let it out slowly.

"I want to fly."

There's a gentle cheer and everyone comes over to hug me, even my mother, who holds me for a long time. The Spirit Flyers watch us for a while. I think one of them is the Spirit Flyer who danced with me in the cornfield at the Midsummer Party last year, since he seems especially happy, but it's hard to tell. They all seem happy, to be honest, even if I am a descendant of one of their disgraced Rogues. They seem to genuinely care that I have joined them, that I will be a Night Flyer for the rest of my life. We all stand and talk for a few minutes. I'm so relieved that my decision is made now. I don't have to worry about it anymore.

But my night of decisions is not over. Soon the lead Spirit Flyer steps forward again.

Gwendolyn Golden, there is one more choice you must make.

We all stop and look at him. I notice that Martin, Jez, and my mom can't look at him very easily. They keep shielding their eyes or turning their heads a little like you would at a bright light, but my little brother and sister stare at him with fascination.

With great sadness, your faithful Watcher, McGovern Everett McGillies the Third, has relinquished his sacred trust as your Watcher due to his illness. All Night Flyers require a Watcher, so you must now choose another to take this special job. Who here will be this Night Flyer's Watcher?

The Spirit Flyer says this to the group and without hesitation, Everton steps up.

"I will. I'll be her Watcher."

I'm so surprised, I try to think of something to say. But I don't have to.

"I will. I'll be her Watcher, too." It's Martin. He steps forward, and for a horrible moment I hope that the Spirit Flyers don't have some weird ancient duel planned for cases like this. But before I can worry too much a third voice says, "I will. I'll be Gwen's Watcher."

And this time it's Jez, my dearest, oldest friend.

All three of them, Everton, Martin, and Jez, stand in front of me.

You must choose, Gwendolyn Golden.

All the joy I've felt for the past two days drains out of me. How can I possibly choose just one of these people to be my new Watcher? I can't do it. I love all three of them in different ways, for different reasons. One old friend, one dear friend, and one new friend. I've been through too much for the Spirit Flyers to make me choose one.

I hesitate for a few moments, but it's impossible. "I choose all three to be my Watcher," I say.

The Spirit Flyers take a few seconds to look at each other, which I think is talking for them.

Yes. It is done. It is amenable, and unprecedented, but we will accept your choice of Jezebel Katherine Fremont, Martin Philip Evells, and Everton Paul Miles as your Watchers. These three friends have brought you joy in different ways, and you have been tried harshly by circumstances beyond your control. We allow it.

The Spirit Flyers lead Jez, Martin, and Everton to a corner of the forest clearing, and I hear each of them murmur as they take the oath to watch over me and generally cover my back for all time.

I sneak off for a moment because I hear my brother and sister giggling in the forest, and I don't want them to wander away. My mom is deep in conversation with Emerson and the other adults. So I slip into the trees and find C2. Christopher is looking with great tenderness at his sister … who is floating just above his head. They both see me, and Christine giggles and waves.

Of course. Of *course* this is how this year will end! How did I not see this coming? Christine was *flying* above the flowers in her picture in Adam's office! Why wouldn't C2 be able to fly, or at least one of them? It makes perfect sense. I smile and wave back. Celestine is suddenly standing beside me, and I think she smiles too (although it's hard to tell).

Little golden sister, your father is all around you.

"I know." I nod. "He really is."

The sacred ring has enhanced your sister's gift on this special night. Do not worry, she is unlikely to fly elsewhere until she is older.

That's a relief. I watch my sister float and listen to the twins giggle in the dark forest for a few moments. Our lives are about to change in ways I can't even imagine. There are two Night Flyers in the family? Possibly three? I can't think about that right now. Not tonight. Instead, I ask something that has been bothering me for a while.

"Celestine, how did you find us in the Shade?"

Do you not know?

"I really don't."

You were the only real heartbeats. The only real love. That is the only way to banish the Shade, with love and with the living. And you two were very much alive.

"Is the Shade gone forever?"

No, little golden sister. There is always sadness, and a new Shade is already on the rise. There will always be a Shade, and other enemies to torment your kind.

"What? What other enemies?"

No, no talk of enemies tonight, Gwendolyn Golden. Now is the time to celebrate.

I want to pester Celestine, who is being unusually cryptic, but the Spirit Flyer moves silently through the trees back to the clearing and the adults. I follow until I have a terrible thought and stop.

"Who's going to tell my mother about my little sister?" Someone is going to have to, and I hope with all my heart that it won't be me. Maybe I can make one of my three new Watchers do it.

Celestine looks at me for a moment.

You are a Night Flyer now, Gwendolyn Golden. Together with your community, there is nothing you cannot face. But tonight I shall help you. I shall tell your mother about your sister's new gift.

A white feather drops from Celestine's wing and drifts softly into my hand with a gentle flutter. My skin receives it with warmth. It feels alive as it settles beside my own golden feather, which I've been clutching.

It is not your father's golden feather, but a Spirit Flyer feather is a rare gift. I am only allowed to give one in my life, and now it is yours. It is a special bond between us. May it serve us both well.

I'm touched. And what does this *special bond* mean, exactly? But the Spirit Flyer is already moving off to the clearing. In the next moment my mother and the crowd of mortals and immortals follow Celestine through the woods toward C2. I can see Everton coming through the trees, looking for me.

The white feather pulses gently in my hand. My mother is about to find out my little sister can fly, and I'm not entirely sure, but I think I've just been adopted by a starshot immortal.

Not strange at all. Just another completely normal day, I'm discovering, if you're a Night Flyer.

And I am.

IN THE SAME SERIES

The Strange Gift of Gwendolyn Golden
Philippa Dowding

One perfectly ordinary day, for no apparent reason, Gwendolyn Golden wakes up floating around her room like one of her little brother's Batman balloons.

Puberty is weird enough. Everyone already thinks she's an oddball with anger issues because her father vanished in a mysterious storm one night when she was six. Then there are the mean, false rumours people are spreading about her at school. On top of all that, now she's a flying freak.

How can she tell her best friend or her mother? How can she live her life? After Gwendolyn almost meets disaster flying too high and too fast one night, help arrives from the most unexpected place. And stranger still? She's not alone.

THE GARGOYLE IN MY YARD

What do you do when a 400-year-old gargoyle moves into your backyard? Especially when no one else but you knows he's ALIVE? Twelve-year-old Katherine Newberry can tell you all about life with a gargoyle. He's naughty and gets others into trouble. But if you're like Katherine, after getting to know him, you might really want him to stay.

Commended for the 2009 Resource Links Best Books, for the 2010 Best Books for Kids and Teens, and shortlisted for the 2011 Diamond Willow Award.

THE GARGOYLE OVERHEAD

What if your best friend was a naughty 400-year-old gargoyle? And what if he just happened to be in terrible danger? Its not always easy, but thirteen-year-old Katherine Newberry is friends with a gargoyle who has lost his greatest friend. Gargoth's greatest enemy is prowling the city, and it's a race against time to find her first!

Shortlisted for the 2012 Silver Birch Express Award.

THE GARGOYLE AT THE GATES

Christopher is astonished to discover that gargoyles Ambergine and Gargoth are living in the park next door and that Katherine, a girl from his class, knows the gargoyles, as well. When the Collector steals Ambergine, it's up to Christopher and Katherine to get her back, as long as something else doesn't catch them along the way.

Shortlisted for the Hackmatack Children's Choice Book Award, the 2013 Diamond Willow Award, and commended for the 2013 White Raven Award.

They're troubling. They're bizarre.
And they JUST might be true …

Weird Stories Gone Wrong

BY PHILIPPA DOWDING

BOOK 1
The ghastly truth about
a giant hand …

BOOK 2
A rainy night,
a haunted highway,
a mysterious monster …

BOOK 3
Are you brave enough to
enter the curious maze?
Not everyone comes out …

*Three tremendously terrifying tales you'll want to share with your
enemies (should you want to scare them silly) …*

Available at your favourite bookseller

VISIT US AT

Dundurn.com
@dundurnpress
Facebook.com/dundurnpress
Pinterest.com/dundurnpress